P9-BJE-451

« Rewind

LAURA DOWER

SCHOLASTIC INC.
New York Toronto London Auckland Sydney
Mexico City New Delhi Hong Kong Buenos Aires

For Richard

If you purchased this book without a cover, you should be aware that this book is stolen property. It was reported as "unsold and destroyed" to the publisher, and neither the author nor the publisher has received any payment for this "stripped book."

No part of this publication may be reproduced, stored in a retrieval system, or transmitted in any form or by any means, electronic, mechanical, photocopying, recording, or otherwise, without written permission of the publisher. For information regarding permission, write to Scholastic Inc., Attention: Permissions Department, 557 Broadway, New York, NY 10012.

ISBN 0-439-70340-9

Copyright © 2006 by Laura Dower

Lines on pages 54, 55, and 56 excerpted from *The Children's Hour*: Copyright © 1934 by Lillian Hellman; copyright © renewed 1964 by Lillian Hellman.

SCHOLASTIC and associated logos are trademarks and/or registered trademarks of Scholastic Inc.

12 11 10 9 8 7 6 5 4 3 2 1   6 7 8 9 10 11/0

The text of this book was set in Walbaum Book.

Book design by Steve Scott

Printed in the U.S.A.

First printing, April 2006

Chapter Twenty-Eight

Prom Night, June 18, 10:25 PM
Cady

Cady Sanchez adjusted her red bra strap and took a deep breath.

Next to her, a serious-looking boy with biceps the size of bread loaves shot a look at a blond girl fixing the T-strap on her sandal.

"We just took this killer stuff," the boy whispered. "Want some?"

The girl twisted her head and glared. "I don't take candy from strangers," she said, shaking her taffeta hips confidently.

Cady watched as the girl headed toward a group of guys and girls singing off-key, a capella, in a corner. Biceps quickly shoved his hands into his pockets to avert the glare of a class chaperone. Orange-carpeted floors vibrated with the heavy boom of DJ Beat's music and the loud pound of more than a hundred feet jumping up and down and up and down.

You know you want it. You know, you know, you know you want it.

The entire school year had been leading up to this?

Most girls had been shopping for their prom dresses since the start of senior year at Chesterfield High School. Now they wandered in and out of the massive ballroom at the Chesterfield Suites like lacy, frosted mannequins, half-dazed with heat, emotion, and the wonder of it all. Cady felt different, looked different, from the rest. Her dress was scarlet; although she didn't wear lipstick or shoes to match, she had painted each toenail the same shocking red.

It had taken Cady all of her seventeen years to get used to most parts of herself, like the downward curve of her nose and the pattern of pale freckles on her right shoulder that looked like a miniature constellation. Her skin was so light, too light, Cady thought, considering that her father was from South America. She wished she looked more like her brother, Diego, whose skin was more olive toned. Cady's light skin came from her mother, Sara, whose own Irish skin was so pale it was almost translucent, like a china doll. Cady didn't want to be anything like china. She didn't want to break.

From inside the ballroom, strobes flashed red, and then yellow. Even from a distance, the disco light pulses gave Cady a headache.

DJ Beat popped his lips and pumped up the volume on one song, a ballad neatly mixed with new wave and rap.

"This one's for Hope," he shouted into the mic.

As soon as Cady heard the name *Hope*, she scanned the faces in the crowd, searching. She hadn't seen Hope White since the start of prom.

The mob of guys from the basketball team (and the mob of girls who liked them) walked by, rapping to one another.

"Hot dress, Sanchez," one player named Darius West called out.

Cady flashed a wide smile. She'd known Darius since

sixth grade, but they'd never been "real" friends. Life was funny that way. You could know people for so long but never know them at all.

"Nice tux, West," Cady whispered. He wore a T-shirt with a picture of a tuxedo on it.

As Darius walked on, Cady glanced at herself in a wall mirror but quickly looked away. What was going on with her hair? The dress was hot and itchy and she already had the makings of a blister on her little toe. And where was Lucas? He'd promised Cady one dance.

But she'd lost him.

Weaving her way through the endless throng of seniors was worse than navigating a driving-test obstacle course. These were the cones and roadblocks of Cady's senior year: the jocks, the jokers, and of course, the beautiful people. Cady narrowly missed knocking a glass of orange punch (definitely spiked) out of one jock's hand. She almost stepped on the open-toed sandal of a girl she hated from music class. Carefully, Cady edged past a cluster of clucking girls who complained about how unfair it was that they couldn't smoke anywhere at the hotel, not even on the outside patio. The hotel had installed cameras to make sure no one broke the rules.

"Cady!" someone cried from the crowd. "Where have you been?"

"Marisol." Cady sighed, relieved to have found one of her friends again. "I was looking for you. Where's Ed?"

Marisol shrugged. "Getting my bag. I think we're gonna go."

Cady tipped her head to the side and squinted. It was

the face she always made when she wasn't so sure about something. "Well," Cady said, "I was thinking of hanging out a little while longer. Just in case. You know."

Marisol grabbed Cady's shoulders. "You look good, girl. You should be working it on some boy who's worth it instead of waiting around for *him*."

Cady laughed. "I don't know how to work it, Marisol. I'm better on backup guitar. Actually, I brought mine with me tonight."

"You did?" Marisol said. "Big surprise. Well, I think it's time you play something loud and kiss that boy's butt good-bye. You know Emile is having a rave later. You're coming, right? Oh—wait—I see Ed. . . ."

Marisol waved to her boyfriend from across the room. Of course they'd only been dating since the winter, but Cady could tell it was true love. Or at least she hoped it was. Cady wanted to believe in true love more than anything. No matter what happened, she was determined to believe.

"Maybe I'll go to the rave," Cady said thoughtfully. "Maybe."

"You better!" Marisol commanded. She gave Cady a "see you later" kiss and hustled away toward Ed.

Cady watched her best friend disappear and scanned the room again. Lucas was still missing. But she spotted a hotel-sized couch along one wall. Sitting down seemed like a good idea.

"Excuse me," Cady said weakly as she squeezed onto the cushions next to a boy named Fly. She recognized him from calculus. His girlfriend, who didn't go to Chesterfield, was at his side.

4

"Mmmnh," Fly grunted. He had crystal blue eyes. Cady couldn't help but stare. His girlfriend looked stoned.

"What are you looking at?" Fly's girlfriend asked.

"Nothing," Cady said, fanning herself with an open hand. "It's just hot."

"Hot," the girl said as she put her hand on the inside of her boyfriend's leg. Without even turning around, Fly slid his hand halfway up his date's skirt, revealing more of her fishnet stockings. They both moaned.

Cady tried not to look. She'd come without a date, and so the sight of two kids feeling each other up made her bristle with utter, total, complete disgust.

And a teeny bit of jealousy.

After all, she'd gone to all this trouble with the red dress.

You know you want it. You know, you know, you know you want it.

The music thumped again. Cady fussed with her long brown hair. She'd stupidly sprayed hair gel into it earlier that evening and now it was sticky like a spiderweb. She could barely comb her fingers through the top.

"Ouch."

Make-out Boy elbowed Cady in the side as he raised his hips and pressed into his girlfriend.

Where was a chaperone when you needed one?

Cady stood up again and walked toward an exit. She needed air.

Through a set of sliding glass doors, Cady wandered onto an enormous mezzanine-level patio and perched over the wide iron railing. She'd begun the night with a group of friends. Now she was alone.

Cady gazed across a field at the main road behind the hotel, tracing the red and white paths of taillights and headlights on cars and trucks moving toward unknown destinations. The traffic made her dizzy. And although the hotel patio was cooler and much quieter than the flashing ballroom, Cady's head still ached.

All around, kids gulped night air and stole French kisses. Cady wished Lucas Wheeler was here, too, with his square shoulders and sweet tongue. Kissing her. She wanted to finger the lock of curly hair that swept across his forehead. She wanted to gaze into his deep-set brown eyes. He always smelled like burned incense and his voice was rough, like he smoked, even though he said he hated cigarettes. He was warm all the time, even in winter.

Everything about Lucas Wheeler was made for kissing.

Prom noise filtered upstairs to guest rooms on the third floor, so hotel security came around with their buzzing walkie-talkies, trying the best they could to keep the rowdiest graduates quiet.

No one was listening.

Students stumbled to the elevator bank, half-drunk with the alcohol they weren't supposed to be drinking. Some headed upstairs to rented suites where they planned to hook up, watch movies, drink some more, and stay up all night long. Others made their way toward the hotel parking lot and lined up for their limousines.

Everyone needed someplace to go, and anywhere was good, as long as it wasn't home. Not yet.

The distressed wooden clock on the mezzanine wall read eleven o'clock. There was still time for Cady to salvage prom. If she hurried. She grabbed the hem of her dress and moved swiftly toward the coat check area. When she got there, Cady leaned into the table, drumming out a song beat with impatient fingertips, and waited for the coat checker to return.

She'd been asked to perform a guitar solo at prom, but all student performances had been cancelled. Now most of the musicians in her class hoped for a late night prom jam, since it might be one of the last times they played together. A group planned to meet at Big Cup, a makeshift coffee house for teens that was set up in the basement of a local art gallery. Cady wished she'd brought her faded jeans and a tee to change into. How was she going to jam in this dress?

"Um, can you hurry it up?" Cady asked the checker, who seemed lost in a maze of bags and coats. "My bag's cowhide with a big silver buckle and it should be sitting next to a guitar case. I mean, how many Fenders are back there?"

Through the loudspeakers, music sped up. There would be a few more fast songs before the end of everything.

Off in the distance, Cady observed a girl standing alone, fingering a blue tassel fringe on a scarf around her neck. Cady guessed that girl had been waiting for a dance since prom began. Sometimes strangers seemed so familiar, Cady thought. Nearby, two other girls jokingly lifted up their shiny tops for just a nanosecond while a cluster of guys applauded. But no one paid much attention to them or their belly-button rings.

Where was the damn bag?

Not so far away, a couple appeared, arguing, just outside

the main doors to the main ballroom. Cady couldn't see the guy at all. He stood hidden behind a pillar. But she knew the girl right away. Cady recognized the low dip in the back of Hope White's long prom dress.

Cady moved her eyes over the curve of Hope's shoulder, down her naked spine, down the V-line of her silk dress, and ending at Hope's slender ankles. Everything about Hope's form was perfectly sewn, buttoned, and zipped. But the poker-straight blond hair was down now, not up, like it had been earlier that night. And Hope's normally eggshell white skin was flushed.

Cady could tell something was wrong.

Then the boy stepped into view.

"Lucas?" Cady said weakly. He waved his arms wildly in the air, as if he and Hope were doing a dance.

But they weren't.

Cady's pulse raced and she edged closer.

"Leave me—" Hope said.

Cady could only hear some of the words.

"Cut the—" Lucas said.

"Don't—"

"Lies—" Lucas cried.

Then he raised his left arm high over his head.

SLAP.

Cady clasped a wide hand over her gaping mouth as Hope fell to the floor.

Lucas didn't move. His jaw clenched. Everyone stopped. Time stopped.

Then someone nearby screamed and the room spun on

its axis. Biceps boy, Darius West and his basketball crew, Fly and his stoner girlfriend all turned.

"Hey!" a guy cried from halfway across the room. "Wheeler, what the hell did you do?"

Jed Baker, one of the biggest kids at Chesterfield, lunged for Lucas.

"You're hamburger, asshole."

A few more guys came over quickly, muscles pumped, knuckles primed.

"Watch out!"

"Did you see that?"

From out of nowhere, another kid tried to sucker-punch Lucas right in the face. Lucas bobbed to the side and stumbled back, coughing.

"Let—me—go—" Lucas mumbled, tugging at his own collar.

But no one let go. The crowd moved in tighter, like a vise.

"What just happened?"

"He hit a girl."

"You piece of —"

"Stand BACK!" a chaperone shouted. "Stand back! NOW!" He clapped his hands.

Reluctantly, the guys pushed away from Lucas, and Cady raced over. She kneeled down beside Hope, who sat on the floor in a crumpled pile, prom dress bunched up around her like purple icing on a dirty cake.

"Oh my God, are you okay?" Cady asked, touching Hope's arm.

"No . . ." Hope said. She touched her own cheek. There was a handprint. "My face . . . burns . . ."

Cady leaned in closer. Her insides were grinding. The whole crowd was grinding.

"Can you stand?" Cady asked Hope.

Another teacher rushed over. "Does someone want to tell me *exactly* what happened here?" she yelled.

Pale yellow organza and floor-length pink satin swooshed as girls hurried to give their own scattered versions of the story. But everything was happening too fast to make any sense.

"Lucas Wheeler just lost it."

"Someone call hotel security."

"Oh my God, oh my God."

Cady squeezed Hope's hand. "Can you stand?" she asked again.

Hope shook her head. "No."

Then Cady looked up, and saw Lucas clearly for the first time. He wiped the corner of his mouth and stared down at his shaking palms.

There was blood on his mouth and hand.

"Oh, shit," Lucas said aloud. "This is bad."

A few more muscle-heads shoved their way toward him, but a chaperone got in the way. "Stand back, I said! Stand back!" he wailed.

The angry crowd moved in and out like it was breathing.

"Just—wait—*please*—let me explain . . ." Lucas said.

Cady saw Lucas thrust his arms into the air,

surrendering to the chaos. She'd never seen him look so scared. His eyes appeared to cross and then uncross like he'd had too much to drink, and Cady guessed that he had. His buddies had probably laced a cup of punch with hard stuff.

"Incident on the mezzanine level. Send up the manager, please."

Out of nowhere, two hotel security guards appeared, pushing through the mob, walkie-talkies in hand. They each grabbed an arm and started to lead Lucas back toward the elevators.

"Hey! Where are you taking him?" a girl yelled.

The taller security guard waved the girl away.

"Out of my way," the guard growled. "This is an accident, and we'll handle it from here. . . ."

"It was no accident!" Hope sobbed, trying to be heard above the crowd. "HE HIT ME!"

"He hit her!" the crowd repeated loudly, eyes rutted with angry judgment.

Cady gazed deep into Hope's eyes, across from her. The truth had to be there. Where was it? Then Cady looked over at Lucas. He stared back, jaw locked. He spoke softly — too softly — to be heard above the din. But Cady could read his lips.

"I screwed up so bad," Lucas said. "It wasn't her. You were the one."

Cady's chest clenched. She knew what he meant.

In one instant, she understood everything.

Cady pulled herself up from the floor and stretched out

the fingers of her left hand. She grabbed at air like she was grabbing for Lucas, even as he was being dragged away by the two security guards. And in spite of everything that had just happened, she still wanted that dance.

She still wanted.

Chapter Twenty-Seven

Prom Night, June 18, 8:12 PM
Hope

Girls crowded around the sink inside the marble bathroom at the Chesterfield Suites. The air reeked of jasmine perfume, baby powder, and antiseptic. A restroom matron sat in a small black leather chair off to one side, passing out hand towels and checking to make sure no one sneaked cigarettes or worse inside the stalls. She had a tip dish on the counter next to her, but it was empty.

Everyone had to pee. The line wound halfway out the door. Girls whispered excitedly about their prom dates or their outfits or, in most cases, about someone else's outfit — and how tacky/ugly/slutty/fill-in-the-blank it was.

"Hey, does anyone have any deodorant?" one girl called out to everyone else in the room.

Hope pressed in front of one sink mirror. She looked up while washing her hands. The pale pink gloss she'd applied an hour earlier had all but disappeared. She spotted Cady Sanchez in the mirror.

"There you are," Hope said, sidling up to Cady. "I wondered if I'd find you."

"You look . . . amazing," Cady said. Her face glowed.

Hope smiled. "Like the dress? It's an original Vance. Dad insisted."

Cady nodded. "Wow."

"Your dress is nice, too," Hope said, stroking the fabric.

Her fingers slid lightly across Cady's wrist. "You really need lipstick, though. Something red hot."

"I put some on when I left the house," Cady said. "But then I forgot to take the tube with me. Dumb, right?"

"I'd give you some of mine, but this is too pale and it just wouldn't go. Sorry," Hope said. She blew a kiss into the mirror.

"So where's your date?" Cady asked. "You come with Rich?"

Hope grinned. "Uh-huh. He's outside with his friends."

"I bet *he* likes your dress," Cady said.

"What's not to like?" Hope countered with a shrug.

"What ever happened to that text-messaging guy?" Cady asked.

"Him?" Hope flinched a little. "Who cares?"

"He stopped texting?"

"Well." Hope paused. "Not exactly. Actually, he might be here tonight."

"Here?" Cady blurted, taken aback. "At prom? Are you kidding?"

Hope shook her head. "He goes to Chesterfield."

"What?" Cady asked, looking concerned.

"I know. I should have told you, Cady. I wanted to tell you. But then I couldn't. Please don't make a big deal . . ."

"Your stalker goes to our school," Cady said with disbelief. "How can you not make a big deal out of that? Who the hell is this guy?"

"Please," Hope said sternly. "Just drop it." She looked around to see if anyone was listening. This whole time she'd led Cady to believe that the "stalker" was a guy from her part-time job over at the medical building, but now the cat was out of the bag — with claws.

"Look, I know you're wondering why I didn't tell you before who this guy is," Hope continued. "And the reason I didn't tell you before and why I'm not telling you now is . . . well . . ." Hope clutched at the garnet stones on a delicate silver choker she was wearing.

"Hope," Cady pleaded, reaching for both of Hope's hands. "You can trust me. Are you scared? I really think we should tell someone. . . ."

Hope looked down at Cady's fingers, now intertwined with her own. Cady's nails were short, with no polish, contrasting starkly with Hope's French manicure. But the two hands fit together nonetheless, like opposing pieces of an interlocking puzzle.

"What's that?" Cady asked, staring at Hope's arm.

Hope looked down. "Nothing," she mumbled. "I bumped into a — "

"Come on. Did *he* do that?" Cady asked. Gently, she pressed her fingertips into Hope's shoulder, and Hope winced dramatically. She'd tried to cover the mark with makeup, but it wasn't hard to tell what lay underneath. This bruise was fresh.

"Hope, talk to me. Now."

"Cady, you have to forget it."

"I can't — "

"Don't — "

"Fine," Cady said, throwing her hands up in the air. "I won't ask you anything else."

Hope took a deep breath and unbuckled the silver sequined clutch that she'd been carrying and slid out a palm-sized bottle.

"Want some?" Hope asked Cady.

"Hairspray? Uh . . . I don't think so."

"Suit yourself."

Hope lifted the bottle and sprayed around her head until every stray hair sat back in place, reprimanded, ready to face the dance. She prided herself on the fact that her hair was always perfect. Hairspray was her force field.

Cady sniffed the air. "Strong stuff," she said. "But it looks pretty good. Maybe I should try a little?" Cady held up a strand of her long dark brown hair and examined it.

Hope lifted the small aerosol bottle and pumped.

"Stop! That stuff really reeks." Cady coughed, fanning the air around her head. She checked her reflection and frowned. "Oh no. Look at me."

"It's not too terrible," Hope said, pasting on a smile. But she knew it wasn't too good either. Cady's hair poked up at the top, and the sides looked like they'd been glued down.

"Maybe he won't notice," Cady said softly, sounding dejected.

"Who won't?" Hope asked.

"You know," Cady said, rolling her eyes.

"Lucas Wheeler."

Hope saw Cady swallow hard. Cady never liked talking about boys, especially not Lucas, and Hope knew that.

"Look, Hope, we're not prom dates or anything, if

that's what you're thinking," Cady said. "Lucas and I said we'd see each other here. That's all."

"That's all?" Hope said.

"Let's quit this, Hope," Cady interrupted. "I know you don't think Lucas is the right guy for me. You've only said that to me like a hundred times. You think he's some kind of freaky loner. I see how you look at him. . . ."

"You do?" Hope said with disbelief.

"Yes, I do." Cady tugged up her bra strap again with determination. "Look, Hope, I know Lucas Wheeler acts a little mysterious, but why do you and everyone else think that makes him some kind of closet . . . *fiend* or something? I mean, what would you do if you had to start a new school for senior year? I know I'd die."

"All I'm saying — all I've ever said — is that Lucas isn't the guy you think he is, Cady."

"Come on, Hope. Is anyone?"

"I know you *think* that the two of you are real friends. . . ." Hope said.

"I don't think. We *are* friends. He gets my music. I can talk to him."

"Like you can talk to me?"

"That's different."

"Incoming!" A girl dressed in a skintight black dress shoved Cady out of the way to get to the sink. Cady nearly toppled over.

"What's your problem?" Hope asked.

"What's *your* problem?" The girl scowled.

Hope nudged the girl so hard that she fell back against the sink.

"Watch it!" the girl shrieked.

"You watch it," Hope said firmly.

"You wrecked my dress."

"Who cares?" Hope said.

"*What* did you say?"

Hope's insides roiled. She wasn't about to let some cow in leather ruin her prom. But before Hope could say anything more, Cady stepped in.

"Come on, let's go," Cady said softly.

The girl backed off and Hope reluctantly followed Cady through the bathroom door.

Prom music pounded hard outside in the hall. Hope glanced around at other seniors decked out in their black and blue and creamy white dupioni silk. Her purple gown stood out in the crowd, although Cady's red dress stood out even more. But was anyone really looking? She searched the crowd for familiar faces.

"This is a good song," Cady said as she moved her hips from side to side. Everything moved except her new helmet hair.

"Oh, look. I see Rich over there by the refreshment table," Hope announced. "I don't see your date, though." She grinned.

"Very funny," Cady said. "I *told* you Lucas isn't my date."

"Yeah, well, good luck," Hope said. "I'm going to go meet up with my other girlfriends now."

"Oh. Will I see you later?"

"I think Emile is having a party at his place. Lots of

booze. Lots of noise," Hope said. "I'll be there, of course. Will you?"

"I was actually going to Big Cup to play some tunes," Cady said. "But I might show up. Later. It depends."

"Yeah, a lot depends on tonight, doesn't it?"

Hope leaned in and gave Cady a kiss. Her cheek pressed ever-so-gently against Cady's for a brief moment before pulling back.

"Oops, I left a mark," Hope said. Laughing, she took a tissue out of her purse and wiped off the pale, smudged lipstick print she'd left behind.

"Stay away from the stalker," Cady said, touching the spot on her cheek where the lipstick had been. "Try to have a good prom."

"You too," Hope said. As she walked away, Hope muttered to herself. "Just don't say I didn't warn you."

Chapter Twenty-Six

June 14, 4:37 PM
Lucas

Lucas stood next to his convertible at the Mobil station, waiting for the automatic pump to click. The armpits on his red faded tee were soaked clear through. He felt moisture between his toes, on his wrists, and the backs of his knees. Summer had finally arrived, stinking of gasoline and sweat.

Of course, it wasn't only the temperature that was making Lucas perspire.

He checked his watch.

In exactly twelve minutes, Hope would leave the doctor's office across the street, where she had a part-time filing job on Wednesdays and Fridays. From there, she would head across Davidson Park, walking quickly toward the deli where she always stopped to buy her cigarettes. She never purchased them at a store where she could be seen by someone familiar. Lucas knew this. He knew a lot of things about where she was going—and where she'd been.

Sure enough, at 4:49, Hope spun through the revolving door at the Gateway Medical Building, her silver cell phone at her ear. She'd gotten highlights the day before and her hair looked lemon-yellow in the sun. She wore a citrus halter top and slim capri pants in deep green, with rhinestone flip-flops. Lucas wondered who she was talking to on the telephone.

He got inside his car, revved the motor, and put the car into gear. Slowly he followed Hope down the street, keeping a safe distance so she wouldn't spot him. At the opposite side of the park, he stopped the car, filled a meter with coins, and quickly dashed into the deli.

He would get there first.

Lucas wandered down the chips aisle, pretending to read the label on a bag of pretzel knots as Hope entered the store. He could hear everything she was saying.

"You saw him?" Hope said into the phone. She picked at the string on her halter as she continued talking. "Yeah, well, my dress was finally altered and you would not believe how good it looks. He's going to melt."

Lucas put down the pretzel bag and walked toward the front of the store. He knew the "he" Hope was talking about was not him.

"Pack of menthols," Hope said to the guy behind the counter, still cleaving the cell phone to her ear. The clerk asked for ID, and she huffed and sighed before finally producing a purple leather wallet embossed with her initials.

Lucas smiled to himself. Of course she had ID. She had a collection of fake IDs.

The clerk handed over the pack of Salems. Hope stuffed them into her bag and clicked her phone shut.

"Hi, Hope," Lucas said, emerging from the chips aisle.

Hope clutched at her chest. "Lucas! Oh, my God. What the hell are you—"

"Surprised?"

Hope's eyelids twitched. She slung her bag over one shoulder and moved toward the deli's front door.

"I have nothing to say to you," Hope said.

Lucas stood in her path. "Nothing?" he asked.

"Stop following me," she said.

"Prom is a week away," Lucas said.

"So? We're not going together," Hope said, steadying herself against a bank of shelves.

"I know you keep saying that," Lucas said, still blocking the way. "But I thought maybe . . . maybe you'd change your mind."

"You just don't get it, Lucas." Hope turned around and started to walk down another aisle in the store.

"But you said it," Lucas said.

"What?" Hope scrambled to get around him.

"*What?*" Lucas asked, eyes flashing.

Hope gasped and turned quickly near the front of the store. As she moved for the door, she knocked over a magazine rack.

"Hey yo! What you do-ink?" the clerk yelled from behind the register. "You read. You buy. What you do-ink?"

Lucas nervously dropped to the floor to pick up the mess. He thought Hope would kneel down to help him, but then realized she'd left the store. The door clanged shut.

Despite the protests of the man behind the counter, Lucas jumped to his feet and pushed the door back open. He saw Hope about fifty yards down the street, trying to run. She couldn't get very far in her flip-flops. As he got closer, she stumbled on a crack in the pavement. Lucas ran over.

"Stay away!" Hope yelled.

"I thought we were going to prom together. I just want to talk about it. I thought—"

"You're delusional," Hope said. "Get a life, Lucas. Seriously."

"I had a life—with you," Lucas said.

Lucas let out a deep sigh and looked up into the vast blue canvas overhead, not a cloud in sight. The breeze was moist like everything else. He smelled the faint odor of Hope's rose-scented perfume. His stomach heaved.

"I know you say it's over, that we're over, Hope, but I still love you."

Hope scrambled to pull herself up off the curb.

"Don't say that word," Hope said. She took a few measured steps back. "I'm going now. Leave me alone. I'm not going to prom with you. I'm not doing anything with you. I told you that a hundred times. I haven't changed my mind. I'll never change my mind."

"If you won't go with me, then who are you going with?" Lucas asked.

Hope's jaw dropped. "Like I'm going to tell you?"

Lucas leaned in and snatched Hope's arm.

"Tell me," he said firmly.

"Lucas, let go. You're hurting me," Hope said.

"Hurting you? How about how you hurt me?" Lucas said. "You can't just say things to people and then pretend like it didn't happen. You've been doing that to me for weeks now."

"Lucas, it didn't happen. Not like you remember it."

Lucas squeezed hard again.

"Let go, Lucas. My arm—"

Hope's voice dissolved into tears as she tried to wrench loose from his grip. But Lucas pinched again, so hard this time that her skin blanched white around his fingers. He would definitely leave a bruise now.

"Stay with me, Hope," Lucas demanded.

"Let me go," Hope begged.

Her eyes darted around the street. She glanced back at the store. She looked across Davidson Park. She searched for someone else on the sidewalk, someone she could call out to. She looked everywhere except directly into Lucas's eyes.

"Look at me," he demanded.

"Let me go," she said again, trying to hold back her tears. "I mean it. Let go now or I will SCREAM."

Lucas held on tighter. Hysteria rose inside of him like seltzer fizz inside a shaken bottle. This was one of those moments his doctor had warned him about back in Boston. It was too hard to keep the lid on when his insides felt like they were trying to bubble out.

Hope's round, blue eyes were like bowls, and Lucas felt himself swimming in them. For a moment, there was a beat of perfect silence between them, a moment of stillness when the truth seemed clear, even if neither person was willing to admit it.

"Hope, I just need — you — "

Across the street a driver slammed on her brakes. Tires squealed. Hope gasped and dropped the bag that was in her free hand.

Part of its contents tumbled out: the menthols, a wrapped tampon, her MP3 player, her Wine-Goes-With-Everything lipstick tube, a pen with the end chewed off, a

24

torn piece of the school newspaper, a ripped photo of Hope and Cady in costume, taken at the school play . . . .

Lucas caught a glimpse of the photo, torn at the corner.

"Cady," he said, his voice just above a whisper.

Almost immediately, he let go of Hope's arm, as if he'd awoken from a trance. He shoved his hands into the pockets of his jeans and ran back in the direction of his car.

"What the hell is your problem?" Hope yelled after him.

Lucas's heart beat hard. His palms were slick. He didn't stop moving until he climbed into the front seat and turned on the car.

Lucas accelerated out of his parking space, but his eyes never really left Hope. He could see her in the rearview, frozen on the sidewalk, surrounded by the objects that had fallen out of her bag.

And as he drove away, Hope got smaller and smaller and smaller still, until she was nothing but a speck on the rear windshield.

Chapter Twenty-Five

June 5, 1:10 PM
Cady

The loudspeakers at the Hancock Mall piped in a bad instrumental version of Elton John's "Candle in the Wind." Cady's head throbbed. She'd taken two Tylenol, but nothing was making the ache go away. It was the caffeine, or rather the lack of it.

"Let's get espresso, Mom," Cady said to her mother as they approached a coffee kiosk. "And I want something super-fattening and frosted to go with it."

"Better be careful, young lady, or you won't fit into your prom dress," Mom said in her singsong voice. "See, your shirt's a little smaller than it was the last time you wore it, isn't it?"

"Thanks for the positive pep talk, Sara." Cady loved bothering her mom by calling her by her first name.

But her mother's comments got Cady thinking. She stopped to check her reflection in a store window. She saw what her mother had been talking about. Cady's peasant skirt was low-slung, and the tie-dyed T-shirt she was wearing had shrunk in the wash. Her belly was showing today, and she hardly ever showed her belly. She wasn't one of those girls with much to show off.

Two guys dressed in army-green shorts and combat boots walked by and nearly crashed into Cady. They snickered as they walked away.

Losers, Cady thought. Coming to the mall sucked even more than going to the dentist. Even the muzak was worse.

Normally, Cady tried to avoid shopping of all kinds, especially in a place like this, with all the pierced posers lurking around. But today she needed shoes — red shoes to match her prom dress — and the mall had the most concentrated selection of shoe stores in a fifty-mile radius. She also needed earrings, some kind of shawl, and a purse, as her mother kept nagging her.

Her mom ordered the two coffees while Cady grabbed a frosted apple fritter, the most sugar-loaded item in the display case. Drinking coffee was more than a pastime in the Sanchez house; it was a religion. Cady's father, Fernando, was originally from Medellín, Colombia, and he bragged that his homeland had *el mejor café del mundo*, aka the best coffee in the world. With Dad, only the best would do.

Sipping their coffees, Cady and her mother walked through the third level of the mall, stopping in front of stores to check out the window displays.

"Let's see. We can try Shoe Land," Cady's mother said, trying to read an illuminated map display located near the main fountain. "Or how about Bewitched? That's a new boutique on the lower level. I think they have cute purses there, too."

"Forget it, Mom," Cady said between nervous bites of her apple fritter. "We'll never find anything to match my dress."

"Don't get all hopeless on me yet. Why don't we look

for the earrings first? The jewelry arcade is right here. I'm sure we can find some cute studs or something."

Cute studs, Cady repeated to herself. *Ugh.*

They slipped through the gilded glass doors of an emporium that offered bracelets, anklets, necklaces, belly chains, and rings at the best prices. Higher-end diamonds and white gold lived on one side of the store. Retro plastic bracelets lived on the other. Cady stopped in front of a case with dangling Indian-style earrings and an assortment of jeweled toe rings.

"You can't be serious," Mom groaned. "You already have at least ten pairs of earrings like these. Daddy and I are getting you a nice pair of rhinestones or something. Not these." A collector of beads from all over the world, Cady's mom made jewelry that she sold to museums, libraries, and specialty shops. She still liked to shop in other jewelry stores for more delicate pieces.

"You're the expert, Mom," Cady replied with a shrug. She normally wouldn't ever choose sparkly jewels to wear for herself, but Mom was buying, and prom only came around once in a lifetime, so she figured what the heck.

As they approached one of the larger display cases, Cady spotted Hope White across the store, modeling a pair of gold hoop earrings for the sales clerk. Hope wore short shorts and platform Skecher sandals that made her tanned legs look long.

"Hope, hey," Cady said softly as she walked up to her friend and slung an arm around her waist.

"Cady? What are you doing here?" Hope said, turning

to Cady with a grin. She pointed to the earrings in her ears. "Aren't these to die for? I don't need them but they look so hot I think I may have to get them. . . ."

Cady nodded. "You look great."

Hope giggled. "That's the idea," she said.

"Hope," Cady's mother interrupted. "I haven't seen you in ages."

"Time flies." Hope nodded.

"Shopping for prom?" Mrs. Sanchez asked.

Hope nodded again.

Cady tugged uncomfortably at her peasant skirt, and the little bells on the drawstring jangled. At moments like this, she wished she were more practiced in the art of meaningless small talk. She wished she were more like Hope.

"What are you shopping for, Cady?" Hope asked. "Last time I saw you . . ."

"I had the prom dress, but that was about it," Cady blurted. "Nothing's changed."

"Yes, I'm afraid we have a few more last-minute things to purchase," Mrs. Sanchez added.

"How can you *not* have shoes yet?" Hope said, linking her arm through Cady's. "Prom is in like five minutes."

"Actually it's in two weeks," Cady said. "And I am seriously considering going barefoot."

Hope forced a little laugh. Cady stared at her friend's teeth. They were so white.

"Why don't you two keep talking while I go look at earrings, Cady? I'll get the saleswoman to pull out a few pairs. We could get rubies if you want."

"Rubies?" Cady asked.

"Yes, they'll look great with your red dress," Mom said. Cady knew her mom liked to talk big, showing off to Cady's classmates, as if that meant something.

Mom wandered off to find the saleswoman on the other side of the store.

"So who's taking you to prom?" Cady asked Hope.

"I still don't know." Hope shrugged. "A couple of guys asked but I just might show up stag. . . ."

"What about Rich from the play?" Cady said.

"Huh? *Him?*" Hope said with a deliberate sigh. "He's dropped way down on my list."

"Oh," Cady said, surprised. After all, she'd seen Hope and Rich together on more than one occasion.

"Wait. You still haven't told me who *you're* going to prom with," Hope said, switching the focus of the conversation like she'd switched on a stage light.

"Well," Cady answered coyly, "no one asked me."

"How is that possible?" Hope said, staring right into Cady's eyes. "You're one of the hottest girls in school."

Cady's skin flushed. "Yeah, right."

"What about Lucas?" Hope asked.

"Who?" Cady asked, caught off guard.

"Stop the act."

"Hope, Lucas and I are strictly friends. I told you."

"Friends — with benefits?" Hope quipped.

"Nonononono. Platonic friends."

Hope raised an eyebrow. "Cady Sanchez, you are the biggest liar on the planet."

"I don't lie," Cady said with a straight face.

"Well, I guess that's a good thing," Hope said. "After all, Lucas Wheeler does sleep around."

Hope's remark hit like the words had been fired out of a gun.

"He sleeps around?" Cady asked.

"Oh yeah," Hope continued. "He and his friends keep this list of conquests. I know this girl who hooked up with him and . . ."

"I don't need to know this," Cady said.

"You should know."

"Why? It's not like he's my boyfriend or anything."

"Well, he is your best guy friend, isn't he?"

Cady stared down at her flip-flops. She wouldn't look Hope in the eye. When had Lucas been messing with another girl? How could Cady have been so stupid?

Hope touched Cady's shoulder.

"Look, Cady, I really, really like you. So please don't be mad at me for telling you all of this. The last thing I wanted to do was hurt your feelings. . . ."

"I should probably go," Cady said softly, cutting Hope off. She quickly searched the room for her mother and caught a glimpse of Mrs. Sanchez across the store, studying the jewelry cases like a private investigator.

Hope didn't seem to register the brush-off. She leaned into Cady and gave her a quick hug. "I just want you to understand the truth and to be all right with it," she whispered. "I know you'd rather know the whole truth."

"Right." Cady gulped.

"I guess there's always a chance Lucas can change," Hope said, trying to sound optimistic.

Cady shook her head. "Whatever."

"Well, here's to rubies," Hope said.

"Yeah, rubies," Cady said, forcing a weak smile.

"Good luck shopping," Hope said.

"You too," Cady said. She pointed to the two gold hoops that dangled from Hope's ears. "You'll be the belle of the ball."

Hope grinned a wide, Cheshire-cat grin. "Nothing less than homecoming queen, right? Ha ha," she quipped, blowing a kiss good-bye. She turned back to the counter to make her purchase.

Cady walked slowly toward her mother. She was grateful for Hope's honesty, but at the same time she felt the air hiss out of her like a pricked balloon. Was everything Hope said true? Lucas *had* been subdividing lately, pieces of himself chipping off each new day. First he couldn't talk to Cady; then he wouldn't talk. He wasn't even writing new music anymore. Despite all that, and despite all the things Hope had just said, a part of Cady still wanted to believe that Lucas Wheeler was the one.

Cady thought back to that time, a month before, at Blue Notes. Lucas had been full of talk, and she'd hung on to his every word like she was scaling some mountain, up to a wide sky, up to him. And just yesterday, Lucas had talked about looking forward to seeing Cady at prom. *Seeing* her. That meant she still mattered, at least a little, didn't it?

Cady didn't know anymore. Something *had* changed. But it wasn't Lucas. It was her. Cady had been so sure of things, and now this sinking, way-way-down-deep-in-her-belly pang of doubt had crept in.

How could Hope White be right about anything? Cady couldn't possibly trust Hope, the same Hope she'd despised for so many years, since elementary school, when Hope rose to the ranks of "most popular" in their class, when Hope had the best hair, the best lips, the best hips, the best *every-thing*. Cady had made a conscious decision to hate Hope White from seventh grade forward. Why change now?

Was it the school play? Cady had been cast with Hope in a production of Lillian Hellman's *The Children's Hour*. The two of them played teachers who get caught in a lie at their school, a lie about the nature of their relationship. It was such an intense story that at moments, Cady felt herself naked, stripped down by its intensity. Although she and Hope still didn't run in the same social circles at school, they discovered a place where their thoughts could safely intersect. Between line readings and run-throughs, an understanding — a bond — was born between them.

"Cady? What about these earrings?"

Her mother held out a beautiful pair of dangling rubies. "Hold these up," she said.

"They're fine, Mom. Let's just get them and go," Cady said. "I don't really care."

"Don't care?" Cady's mother made a face. "Since when do you not care? What's eating you?"

"I'm just tired," Cady said stiffly. "Let's go check out that Bewitched place. Like you said, we can get shoes and a bag at the same time. It's late. We have to go pick up Diego at lacrosse, right?"

Cady's mother draped her arm around Cady's shoulder and pressed in close.

"I know what you're thinking, Cady," she whispered. "You're stressed about prom."

Cady's mother liked to pretend like she could read her daughter's mind.

"You need to stop your worrying. You're going to be a knockout," Mom continued. "And you're so much prettier than that Hope White."

Cady smiled. "No, I'm not. But thanks anyway, Mom."

As they left the jewelry arcade arm in arm and headed for the shoe store, Cady caught a glimpse of Hope again, window-shopping on the mall tier below. Cady paused at the railing. She couldn't avert her eyes.

"What's going on?" Mom asked, putting her arm on Cady's back.

Cady wanted to admit everything—everything—right there to her mother: about Hope, about Lucas, about all the things that had happened since that New Year's party.

But she didn't. She couldn't.

Cady wasn't sure what was going on inside her head anymore.

Chapter Twenty-Four

June 1, 4:26 PM
Cady

It was only the first day of June, but summer was already here. The temperature inside Chesterfield High School had reached almost eighty degrees during the day. It was a relief to finally get outside once classes had ended.

Cady walked out into the front courtyard of the school carrying her guitar case. Her thick hair *always* made her feel just a little bit bigger than she really was, but this was ridiculous. She swept the massive frizz up onto her head with a large black clip and hiked up her jeans. Cady liked the way low-rider denim hugged her hips, but she hated how the jeans always felt like her butt was about to fall out. Plus, with the heat, everything felt doubly sticky. Thankfully she was wearing her new white eyelet peasant top. It looked and felt cool.

"Steamy enough?" Lucas called out from across the courtyard.

Cady laughed. "That's the understatement of the century. Check out my hair."

"Some like it hot," Lucas replied lazily, fanning himself with one hand.

Even with the warm weather, Lucas wore a long-sleeved, wrinkled white oxford shirt with the sleeves rolled up, of course; jeans that were faded in all the right places;

and a ripped-up pair of green Chuck Taylors. But he wasn't all calm and collected. Hair curled off his face in a wide cowlick that made him look like a wild-eyed little boy and revealed the bump on his forehead from a collision on the soccer field a week earlier.

"Didn't you say to meet at four?" Lucas asked, scratching his arm as he walked over. A long scar stretched from wrist to elbow on his left arm. An unfortunate accident with a fence was how he explained that one.

Since the night they first met, Cady had been counting Lucas Wheeler's scars. He had them all over his body. According to Lucas, he'd been burned, cut, and slashed more than eleven times in his seventeen years. He'd even impaled one part of his leg with a kabob skewer during a class barbecue back when he was attending school in Boston, long before he came to Chesterfield. That had left a dime-sized knot of tissue on the skin's surface. For Lucas, no scar came without its story.

"Sorry I'm late, but I had to meet with Mr. Guiney and you know how that goes." Cady grinned. Their mutual math teacher got a perverse pleasure out of explaining calculus sets in excruciating detail.

"Whatever," Lucas said, scrunching up his eyebrows like he was thinking hard. He was one of those guys who had imperfect bushy eyebrows. *At least*, Cady thought, *he doesn't have a unibrow.*

"I can't believe how much work I missed because of the play, Lucas," Cady sighed, even though Lucas wasn't looking at her anymore. "I have to take this make-up test or Mr. Guiney's going to lower my grade even though I aced the midterms. Plus, I missed a whole section in my English class and now we have a paper due, and . . . um . . . Lucas?"

Lucas still wasn't looking at Cady. He stared straight ahead.

"Lucas?" Cady asked again.

"Huh?"

"Where did you go?"

"Go?" Lucas asked.

"I'm standing here raving like a village idiot and you're spacing out on me."

"Oh. Sorry."

Lucas turned back toward her, but Cady could tell that his mind was still elsewhere. It wasn't anything new. For weeks, really months, now, he'd been harder to talk to.

Wordlessly, Cady and Lucas reclined on the low brick wall that edged the school yard. The grass was neatly trimmed. A can near the wall overflowed with soda bottles and bees buzzing around for a few good pieces of trash. On the ground, Cady saw a bright blue, torn piece of paper. She recognized the flyer for the school play that had just ended, and that she'd been in.

Lillian Hellman's
The Children's Hour
Chesterfield Auditorium B
8 PM
May 8, 9, and 10
Tickets $6 at the door

Cady leaned over and crumpled the paper. She aimed for the trash can but missed. Lucas jumped up and pretended to do a slam dunk.

"So, do you have a tux yet?" Cady asked.

"Huh? A what?"

"Tuxedo. For prom."

"Oh. That."

Cady smiled. She felt her cheeks flush a little. She and Lucas had talked before about maybe going to prom together — just as friends, they said, of course — but they had never made a real decision whether or not to do it. Cady kept trying to bring it up. Although she told Lucas she was interested in going with other boys, Cady wanted to go to prom with Lucas. Only Lucas.

"Remember the prom dress we saw in the window of that store last month?" Cady asked him. "The red vintage taffeta one with the low neckline?"

"Taffeta prom dress? Nah." Lucas grunted.

Cady tried not to act disappointed. She nudged him. "Come on," she prodded. "You remember. You said I'd be the best-looking girl at prom: a real babe in drop-dead red. You don't remember saying that?"

"Maybe," Lucas said with a sly smirk. "Sounds a little like something I'd say."

"Well, I bought it. It's hanging in my closet, ready to dance."

The school doors clanged as a group of students came outside. Members of the photography club gathered on the nearby lawn with their cameras and tripods and other assorted equipment, trying to find the right angles behind the shadows, backs to the sun. One kid aimed his camera at Cady and Lucas, and Lucas held his flat palm up in front of his face.

"No candids, man," he said.

"But it's for a special issue of the school paper," the boy replied, still aiming his 35-millimeter lens in their direction. "Last one of the year."

Lucas growled. "No way."

Cady giggled. "Come on, Lucas. It's no big deal."

"Look, I don't like pictures," Lucas groaned, putting his head down between his knees so the photographer had no possible shot.

"Dick," the boy said under his breath as he lowered his camera and walked away. Lucas ignored him.

"What is wrong with you?" Cady asked.

"Me?" Lucas said.

"You're being so . . . so . . ." Cady said.

"So?"

"Antisocial weird."

Lucas rolled his eyes toward the sky. He leaned backward and stretched out on the wall, hands cupped behind his head like a pillow.

Cady looked out at the parking lot. A guy tossed a basketball and made a shot. It hung on the rim for about ten seconds before dropping through the net. As it dropped through, a large blackbird let out a screech in the trees near school.

Cady jumped. So did Lucas. "What the hell *was* that?" he said, leaping up from the wall.

"Crow," Cady said plainly, still looking up at the tree.

She fingered the handle of her guitar case, which was propped up on the wall next to where she and Lucas sat.

"What are you doing this weekend?" Lucas asked.

"I have a paper due," Cady sighed. "My little brother has a lacrosse match. And I'm working on that new song I told you about. I've rewritten it about twenty times already."

"Smooth," Lucas said. "You finally get your guitar restrung?"

Cady nodded. "Yeah, for the second time."

Lucas licked his lips and Cady caught herself staring. Today he wore a small turquoise charm around his neck on a thin black leather cord. She could just barely see it between the open buttons of his shirt. The charm looked familiar, but she'd never seen him wear a necklace before. Then again, she'd only seen Lucas once with his shirt unbuttoned all the way.

The crow cawed again and Lucas looked up toward the tree.

"Get lost, bird!" Lucas yelled.

He picked up a rock and threw it up where the bird had been sitting on a long branch. Leaves rustled as the rock whizzed past.

"What are you doing?" Cady asked.

"Target practice," Lucas replied.

The bird's wings flapped madly. It took off into the air.

"I can't believe you did that," Cady said.

"Aw, Cady, please don't lecture me with all your save-the-animals, granola crap," Lucas groaned.

"Crap? I thought you felt the same way as me."

"Whatever."

Lucas stared off into space again. His knees bounced up and down like a car motor revving. He was ready to take off; Cady could tell. Lately, Lucas always made a swift exit, a lot like a startled bird. Whenever he and Cady were together, he was always the first to fly away.

Cady grabbed her straw bag with one hand and tugged it over her shoulder. Then she picked up her guitar case. What would happen if today *she* left first?

"Where are you going? Come on, Cady, I was only joking around," Lucas said.

Cady didn't move.

"Did I tell you that you look nice today?" Lucas said.

"No." Cady made a face. "You didn't tell me that."

Lucas stared right at Cady, and she couldn't contain the flutters in her stomach. Sometimes all Lucas had to do was cock his head a certain way and she was gone. Cady sat back down on the wall alongside him, now.

"Have you thought any more about us going to prom?" Cady asked. "Seriously."

"Yeah, I've thought about it, but the truth is I don't know if I'm going," Lucas said.

"Huh?"

"I know what we said about renting a limo and getting all dressed up and how it would be fun to go and make fun of everyone else." Lucas sighed. "But that was just talk, right? I mean, things change."

Cady paused. "Things . . . change?"

"I might still go . . ." Lucas said.

"Might?" Cady said.

"You could save me a dance—just in case," Lucas said.

"Save you a dance?" All at once, Cady's flutters evaporated. Anger moved in. "I can't believe you, Lucas Wheeler," she said slowly, carefully. "You play this game all semester and now you want me to just forget all the things we said. You want me to sit around all prom waiting for you to get there so you can pity-dance with me once—maybe—and then drift off to smoke weed with your stupid soccer friends?"

"Whoa. Harsh," Lucas said, throwing his hands up like a boxer. "Be fair."

"Fair?" Cady laughed. "I swear. I don't know you anymore."

"Maybe you *don't* know me," Lucas mumbled.

"What happened?"

"I don't know, Cady. Life happened."

Cady felt her chest tighten. Now he was feeding her lines from some crappy soap opera. This wasn't a real conversation. She had to go.

But as usual, Lucas was the one who stood up to leave first. He picked himself up off the wall, brushed bits of grass and dirt off his jeans, and shoved his hands into his pockets.

"You don't want to go to prom with me, Cady," Lucas said bluntly.

"How do you know what I want?" Cady asked.

"Look, I can't keep track of your problems. I have my own."

Lucas shook his head and started to walk away. Cady wanted to grab his arm and tug him back toward her. But she just stood there like a totem pole, jaw open, arms at her side.

"What problems?" Cady whispered under her breath as she watched Lucas walk away, wishing she could crawl inside his head, wishing she knew what it was exactly that had changed between them, wishing she could just . . . speak.

From up in the tree, the crow cawed again.

It was back.

Cady wondered when Lucas would come back, too.

Chapter Twenty-Three

May 20, 3:08 PM
Lucas

"Give me five more, Meulbauer!" Coach Sipkin called out.

The soccer team broke into a chorus of laughter as their teammate, Wesley Meulbauer, jogged around the playing field, arms extended like an airplane.

"Go, Wes!" Lucas called out, fist pumping the air.

"Shut up, Wheeler, or you're next," Coach barked at Lucas.

Everyone stifled the laughs and turned their attention back to the scrimmage.

The Chesterfield Hornets were practicing for one of their final matches of the season. Everyone was distracted, especially the seniors. School was practically over for the summer. Most kids knew where they were heading for college, *if* they were heading for college. What was the point of grades anymore? What was the point of paying attention? The only thing worth fighting for these days was a hotly contested soccer match against the Rockwell Wolverines, the team across town. Right now, the teams were running neck-and-neck for the distinct honor of third place in the district.

Coach Sipkin had the team get into penalty shot formation. "Get back over here, Meulbauer," he called down the field. Wesley hurried over to join the rest of the team.

Jed Baker was penalty-kicking today, as usual.

"You kick that soccer ball like a cannonball, son!" Coach Sipkin always said. Jed was Chesterfield's secret weapon.

Five of the guys on the team lined up. Lucas stood on the end, guarding Wesley. They engaged in a shoving match, back and forth and back and forth until Coach blew his whistle and called them off.

"Where's my goalie?" Coach cried. His face puffed red around the nose and cheeks. He blew his whistle again. Everyone turned around to look at the goal net. Goalie Sean Duncan was doubled over.

"DUNCAN!" Coach yelled. He furrowed his brows. "WHAT IS YOUR PROBLEM, SON?"

Duncan wasn't tying his shoes or monitoring the grass. Even from a distance, he looked a little green. Coach ran over to help. He brought two other guys with him.

"Look who showed up for practice again," Jed said as soon as Coach was out of earshot. He pointed toward the bleachers.

Lucas turned. A group of girls lingered on the sidelines with cell phones to their ears, wearing tube tops, shorts, and designer track shoes. They hung out mostly when the tanning was optimum. Today was an SPF-15 day.

Hope White stood at the edge of the pack.

Lucas raised his hand into the air to wave to Hope, but quickly dropped his arm and thought better of it. There would be another time to win back her attention, but not here. Not now.

Not in front of these guys.

"Check it out," Jed Baker said. "It's the party posse."

"Yeah, easy street," another guy laughed. He high-fived Jed.

"Yo!" Jed yelled. He made a kissy face and shook his rear.

Lucas saw all the girls, including Hope, make kissy faces back. Hope blew on her hand. Lucas chuckled. He figured that what Hope was *really* saying was KISS OFF.

"You boys see what Lenora is wearing today?" Jed continued.

"Yeah, I'll take some of that," another guy said.

"Me first," Wesley said with a smile, clapping his hands together.

"Like *any* of you know what you're talking about," Lucas muttered.

"Luke, we *know* the deal," Jed said with a wink. "Believe me. BELIEVE me. Man, you ain't seen nothing until you see how these girls purr at the end of the season. You weren't at Chesterfield last year."

"Last year?" Lucas echoed, giving the guys a confused look. "What about last year?"

Wes explained. "Soccer party after the final match. Everyone was . . ."

"Hot, hot, hot!" some guy said, chuckling.

"Maybe this year we'll get a repeat performance," Jed said.

The rest of the group let out a loud, "Ree-peat! Woo-hoo!"

"What are you morons talking about?" Lucas asked.

The tips of his ears burned. His eyes flashed. "Why don't you guys just leave those girls alone —"

"Hey, what are you? Their guardian angel?" some guy snapped.

The other guys snickered.

"Come on, Luke," Jed said. "It's the end of senior year and you're still — STILL — the new kid? Aw, man. You don't know jack." Jed raised his hand and motioned over to the group of girls again. One of the girls — not Hope but a brunette with auburn highlights — beckoned Jed with a crooked finger, and hiked up her revealing miniskirt. Then she laughed at her own tease. The rest of the girls laughed, too, even Hope.

"STAND UP, DUNCAN!"

Lucas quickly glanced down toward the goal. Coach Sipkin stood over the goalie, Duncan, clapping his hands onto the boy's back. Obviously Coach couldn't hear Jed or any of the others from his downfield position.

Jed didn't seem to care either way. He shook his backside for a second time.

"Yo, Pam!" he yelled to the brunette. "You want some?"

Pam wagged a finger back at Jed. "You wish!" she yelled back.

"Then what *do* you want?" Jed asked.

"Not you, Baker!" Hope shouted louder than everyone else.

The girls laughed out loud. The guys laughed even louder.

"Oh, that hurts!" Wesley said.

Jed pretended to be shocked. He turned to the other guys, shook his hand to the side, and wiped imaginary sweat off his brow. "Is that Hope White tight or what?"

"Yeah, man," Lucas said. "She nailed you."

"Truth is, Wheeler, I nailed her."

Lucas tightened one fist and clasped the opposite hand over it, ready to punch. Jed had gone too far.

But before Lucas could act, the group of girls lifted their hands into the air simultaneously and waved a Queen of England wave to all the guys on the soccer team. Then they shuffled a little farther down the field, their chests thrust out.

For Hope, flaunting assets wasn't too hard. She was the curviest of the bunch. Lucas watched Hope's hips slide from side to side as she and the rest of the group walked away.

"What the hell was all that about?" Lucas asked Wesley.

"You know," Wes said. He flung his arm over Lucas's shoulder.

"No, I don't," Lucas said.

"Those girls are into serious fun this time of year," Wesley explained. "You know what I mean."

Lucas still had his fists clenched. "No, I don't know." He knew that most guys found Hope attractive, but he had no idea . . .

"Have you been living in a cave, Lucas?" Wes asked. "The party posse delivers after prom. It's a Chesterfield tradition."

"Delivers? I can't believe . . ." Lucas's voice trailed off. He stared over at the girls again. "*All* of them?"

"Yeah," Wesley said. "Mostly."

"Jesus," Lucas answered in a flat monotone.

Hope couldn't be a part of the posse, could she? His gaze lingered on her from afar. He could still make out the line of her slim waist and the texture of her spandex top. He imagined touching her here, there, under, over, and in between.

"What, do you have a thing for one of the girls?" Wes asked, arching his brows. "Is that it?"

"No."

"Who? Tell me. Lenora? Pam?"

"No," Lucas said emphatically.

"Hope?"

Without even thinking, Lucas looked down at the ground. It was a dead giveaway.

"How long have you liked her? I don't want to be harsh, but seriously, does Hope White even know you exist?"

"What the hell is your problem?" Lucas snapped. "Just drop it."

"Chill," Wes said, sensing Lucas's anger spike. "I'm just playing."

Lucas resisted the desire to grab Wes by the throat. He remembered the time his Navy dad had tried to tell him the exact spot where a person could press and snap someone's neck. But this was no place for neck snaps. Lucas shook his own head coolly and took a step back.

"Let's get this straight. I don't have a thing for anyone, Wes," Lucas said slowly and deliberately. "You need to stop saying shit that isn't true, okay? *Okay?*"

"Okay, Lucas. I was kidding around. It's just some girl."

Lucas rolled his eyes and moved away. He needed to put distance between himself and this conversation, pronto.

Early on in the school year, Lucas had been designated "the new senior hottie" by the *Chesterfield High Reporter* in a school poll on new students. But Lucas hated the nickname. He hated labels. And since then, he had made a promise to himself that he would not talk to guys like Jed or Wes about girls, especially not girls like Hope White. In fact, he tried not to talk about anything important when he didn't have to.

As far as Lucas Wheeler was concerned, all anyone at school needed to know about him was that he'd moved to town from Boston with his dad. He had no brothers or sisters. He had a German shepherd mix named Boo Radley. He was good at math. He could play a mean lick on his Gibson. And he played left wing on the soccer team.

Only two people knew more than those basics. And what Cady Sanchez and Hope White knew, they knew for different reasons.

With Cady, it made sense for Lucas to share certain parts of himself: the music parts. Lucas and Cady both wrote songs, and being a songwriter meant being honest — at least some of the time. A song was like a promise.

But with Hope, there were no limits. Long ago Lucas decided that he needed to share *everything* with her.

And he had.

There was only one problem with doing that. Lucas had never dreamed of a day when Hope would ignore his calls, his text messages, or his e-mails. He'd never imagined her avoiding his looks in the halls at school.

Fweeeeeeeeeeeeeeeeeeet!

Coach Sipkin blew his whistle loudly.

"Hustle up, chumps!" Coach cried. "Let's finish this up right now. Duncan's fine. Baker, kick it. We're behind schedule, boys!" He clapped his hands again. "Move it! Move it! MOVE IT!"

The guys barely had a moment to get lined up before Jed went for the soccer ball.

POP! It whizzed through the air like it really had been shot out of a cannon. The only problem was that Jed had missed his target, and the ball flew directly into the lineup of his teammates.

Lucas briefly saw the ball—or rather, the blur—before it hit him in the head.

But in a split second, he was facedown on the ground.

Coach Sipkin blew his whistle a few more times and jogged over to Lucas, who rolled onto his back, stunned.

"Out of the way, boys!" Coach barked as he kneeled on the ground and grabbed Lucas's wrist. "Pulse, check. Breathing, check. Can't you boys do anything without getting sick or hurt today?"

"What's going on?" Lucas reached up to touch the top of his head, but missed. He was dizzy.

"Nice kick, Jed," Coach said.

"It's a practice, Jed," Wes growled. "You didn't have to kick so hard."

Jed shrugged. "Hey, man, it's a game. Lucas should have gotten out of the way."

Off in the distance, the group of girl soccer group-ies — including Hope — looked on, seemingly intrigued by the accident.

"Hey, Lucas, they're looking this way again," Jed whis-pered down into Lucas's ear. "Check it out. I bet they all want you."

Wes laughed out loud.

"You son of a —"

Lucas swung for Jed's head but missed his target com-pletely and fell back onto the grass. He tried craning his neck, but the pain pinched even more when he moved it.

"Ouch," he groaned. His head throbbed, but he swal-lowed the hurt. Why couldn't he shake off this fog? Lucas tried again to twist his head but winced with the sting.

He couldn't see downfield. He couldn't see her.

Hope was gone.

Chapter Twenty-Two

May 8, 10:11 PM
Cady

Cady fancied herself more musician than actress. It was Lucas who convinced her to audition for *The Children's Hour.* He was always daring her to do wild things, and Cady liked it when Lucas gazed at her with wide-eyed astonishment—and approval.

Cady had started playing guitar when she was six. Her mother had sent her out of the house for real music lessons so Cady would stop playing drums on every mixing bowl and pot in the kitchen, destroying both them and the spoons, spatulas, and other makeshift drumsticks in the process. In these lessons, Cady would play chords over and over again to get them just right. Within weeks, her fingers were calloused on the tips. The teacher held a concert for parents, and Cady was the star pupil. Although she did well in the spotlight, something about it always made her feel edgy.

But here she was, front and center again, thanks to Lucas. Thanks to a senior year that had turned out unlike any school year she'd ever known, Cady was one of the leads in the school play. She and Hope were both playing the parts of teachers, Hope as Karen and Cady as Martha. And to Cady's own surprise, she loved it.

Before the final act of the play's final performance, Cady found herself alone backstage, just as she had during the other performances and rehearsals, standing behind one of the thick, heavy, velvet curtains. The stage was set with heavy parlor furniture on one side and a kitchen counter and appliances on the opposite side. Of course, the appliances were mostly painted wood. The setting was supposed to be the apartment where Cady and Hope's characters lived.

From her spot in the wings, Cady could just barely see the play's action. Actors moved from stage left to right and back again like a broom, their voices deep and serious.

In her hand, Cady clutched a wheat penny. It was one of the Lincoln pennies minted before 1959. Lucas had given it to her for luck, and she'd carried it in her pocket throughout all the performances. Cady's hands sweated as she passed the coin from palm to palm, taking short, shallow breaths and running over the lines for her final scene inside her head. The stage manager rushed up behind Cady and grabbed her shoulder.

"You're back on in two minutes, Cady," she said. "Places."

Cady nodded and headed for her entrance mark. As she turned, the penny slipped out of her hand and clinked onto the floor. "Ooh!" Cady let out a gasp. Then she rolled up the sleeves of her rose-colored cardigan sweater set, got on to her hands and knees, and began to search for the coin in the dark. All she found were dirt and dust bunnies at the curtain hem.

"I'll be coming back," the character Joe Cardin said aloud.

Cady knew her cue. She jumped up and tossed her shoulders back, brushing the dirt off the long, plaid wool skirt that her character wore. Blood rushed back into her head. She pinched herself for luck since she didn't have the penny anymore. One more line and she would glide onstage center.

"Never, darling." Hope's voice was clear and slow.

That was it.

Cady entered as Martha.

"It gets dark so early now," Cady said, looking around furtively. The character of Martha was supposed to be high-strung, nervous. That seemed about right for Cady these days.

She continued her fast-paced dialogue. "When the hawks descend, you've got to feed 'em," Cady said. "Where's Joe? Where's Joe?"

"Gone," Hope responded.

The two girls continued to act for a while on automatic pilot. But when they got to the part just before Martha made her final exit, Cady began to feel a wave of dizziness. Words felt thick like glue in her mouth. It was as if Martha had slipped under Cady's skin and down her throat.

"It's funny; it's all mixed up. There's something in you and you don't know it and you don't do anything about it. . . ."

Cady said Martha's words from the play as if they were her own. She continued through her monologue, on to her last lines.

"Tomorrow? That's a funny word. We would have had to invent a new language, as children do, without words like tomorrow."

When Cady looked up, Hope was weeping. It was the

proper stage direction, but tonight something about Hope's tears seemed real.

Cady slouched sadly offstage for the last time. The stage manager squeezed her forearm and gave her a high five that nearly knocked her off her feet. The scene had left Cady unsteady for some reason.

Plock.

Out in the auditorium there was a pall of silence. There always was silence after the gunshot. Martha had gone offstage to kill herself, grimly enough. Cady hated that about her character — the giving up part. Cady never wanted to give up like that in her own life.

As Hope recited the very last word of the play, "Goodbye," a few students in the audience shouted out the names of various cast members. Before long everyone was standing. Applause crested as the final curtain pulled shut like a crashing wave, muffling all sound for a brief moment.

The cast waited. It was all hot breath and whispers behind the dark curtain.

Hope reached out for Cady's fingertips and Cady pulled back a little because her hands were still shaking and sweating from the scene.

"You did it. We did it," Hope said. "I don't know what I would have done if you hadn't been here."

"Well . . ." Cady wasn't sure what to say. "I don't know . . . I mean . . . you . . ."

Hope leaned in and softly kissed Cady's cheek.

Cady didn't move.

"I don't know why we haven't been better friends until now," Hope said. Her voice was syrup. She reached up toward Cady's hair — and then traced a trail down Cady's cheek with one finger. "You mean a lot to me, Cady, and I'm not just saying that."

Cady didn't hear any of the audience sounds from behind the curtain. She didn't hear her cast mates giggling and sighing and congratulating one another. When Hope spoke, Cady heard only Hope's voice. She saw Hope's face framed with the red light from the buzzing backstage EXIT sign. She saw Hope's lips.

"You mean a lot to me, too."

All at once, the heavy curtains tugged back, nearly knocking cast members over like bowling pins. Everyone began to laugh with relief. The play was over, really over. In a flash, the house lights went up. The cast marched back onstage, hand in hand, to take their bows. Music swelled from the auditorium speakers.

As Cady and Hope took their individual curtain calls, Cady heard her friends Marisol and Bebe woof like a pack of dogs in the audience.

"Cady! Cady!" they cried.

Cady grinned knowingly and wondered if Lucas was out there, too, whistling and rooting. He'd promised to come to this final performance, but Cady wasn't entirely sure how good his promises were these days. Although she tried to spot his tall frame in the crowd, Cady realized that she'd just have to wait to see if he showed up backstage.

The dressing room was crammed with parents carrying crushed bouquets of "we're oh-so terribly proud of you" flowers, teacher advisers, students from all grades, musicians, and actors. Some of them had attended all three of the sold-out performances. They jockeyed for position near the mirrors where actors removed clothes and makeup and exchanged hugs and kisses.

"This is a madhouse," Cady said, looking around.

"This is so fake," Hope declared.

Cady was surprised. "Why do you say *that*?"

"Listen to them. No one here is really going to stay friends after the play is over. It's all just a big act."

"You don't know that," Cady said. She wondered if Hope was talking about everyone else or really just about herself.

Hope turned toward Cady. "In case you were wondering, I wasn't talking about you and me," Hope said.

For a fleeting moment, Cady believed in mind-reading.

"Faaabulous job, girls!" Ms. Wagner, the director, said as she came up behind the two girls. She clapped them both on the back at once. "This might just be the best show we've ever produced at Chesterfield."

Hope smiled wide. "Of course it was the best."

Ms. Wagner toddled away.

"Gee, thanks for the memories, Fat Ass," Hope sneered under her breath.

"You're awful," Cady said, stifling a laugh even though she did think it was a funny thing to say. She wasn't a big fan of Ms. Wagner herself.

"It's getting late. I have to go change," Hope said, standing up abruptly with a few tugs to her wool costume. "And I have to piss so bad."

Cady laughed again, but uncomfortably this time. She hated that word. *Piss.*

People shoved and crowded into corners to hug their kids or cousins or their best friends. Random parents slid by and pinched Cady's shoulder with compliments and congratulations. Where were *her* mom and dad? Carefully, Cady made her way over to a free mirror and plucked off her false eyelashes and applied cold cream to her cheeks.

"*¡Mi hija!*"

Cady spun around and came face-to-face with her parents.

"*¿Cómo estas?*" Dad asked, scooping Cady into his arms and planting a kiss on her cheek. No sooner had he kissed her than he realized that he had gotten a mouthful of cream.

Cady giggled.

"You'll forgive me if *I* don't kiss you," Mom said, gesturing to the cream on Cady's face.

"I'm so glad you both came," Cady said. "Where's Diego?"

"Oh dear," Mom said.

"That boy," Cady's father blustered.

"Diego crashed the car," Mom stated plainly.

"*¡Mi coche hermoso!*" Dad groaned, and threw his hands into the air.

"Oh my God. Is he hurt?" Cady asked.

Mom shook her head. "No, just grounded. It was only a fender bender. Sorry to worry you, sweetheart. And we should be talking about the play, not your brother."

"Yes, let's not waste our breath," Cady's dad said. "I don't have time for such nonsense."

Cady forced a smile. "Well, I'm glad Diego's okay."

"We all are," Mom said. Cady could tell her mom wanted to change the subject. "So, where's your costar?"

"Hope just went into the bathroom," Cady explained. "And I'll probably be a while. You want to wait in the lobby while I change?"

After more hugs and kisses, Cady's parents shimmied back through the crowd, and out the large doors to the main auditorium.

"I want an autograph," a boy behind Cady demanded, his voice playful.

Cady whirled around to see Lucas holding up a bouquet of beautiful white lilies, purple irises, and pink freesia.

"Magnificent, Cady. Truly."

Cady took the flowers.

"Thanks," she said sweetly, relieved to see Lucas's smile. It almost made her forget all about how much he'd changed lately and how they'd had that terrible fight in the library a few days before.

"So . . ." Lucas said expectantly.

"I'm glad you came," Cady said, dabbing at her face with a damp baby wipe from a container on the counter. "I knew my parents would be here tonight. I was just hoping *you* wouldn't miss the show."

"Miss this? I don't think so," Lucas said. "I owe you."

Cady sighed. "So what did you think — *really* think?" she asked.

"I was a little bummed about the ending, even though I guess I saw it coming," Lucas said. Then he smiled. "I was absolutely blown away by your acting, Cady. I told you that you would kick. Was I right or was I right?"

60

"R-right," Cady stammered. "I-I guess." She reached for her cheek. It was hot.

"Are you blushing?" Lucas asked, swaying forward, hands stuffed tight into the pockets of his button-fly jeans.

Cady looked away nervously.

"No," she said.

"There sure are a lot of drama wonks back here," Lucas said, his eyes scanning the room.

"Wonks?" Cady chuckled. "Shhh. They'll hear you."

"Like I care what anyone thinks," Lucas replied softly.

Cady turned back to the mirror and wiped off the other side of her face. In the reflection she saw Hope walking back from the bathroom.

"Uh-oh, here comes your favorite person," Cady said sarcastically.

"Excuse me," Hope snapped at Lucas when she saw him.

"Right," Lucas stammered. He stepped away from Hope.

"Lucas says everyone was cheering for us in the audience," Cady said to Hope. "Lucas says we were great."

"I know we were great, Cady," Hope replied, staring back at her own reflection. "I don't need some guy to tell me that."

Lucas shuffled even farther to the side, hands still in his pockets, and rocked from heel to toe. Cady could sense his discomfort.

Someone on the opposite side of the dressing room flagged down Lucas so he went over to say hello. Cady watched as Hope reapplied her lipstick and touched up her eyeliner.

"I can't believe it's over," Cady said with a sigh.

Hope looked up at Cady in the mirror. "Everything ends," she said, glaring.

The glare shot through Cady like a laser beam. Why was Hope acting so cruel when a moment before she'd been so . . . *gentle* . . . with Cady onstage, alone? Was Hope jealous about the fact that a guy — any guy — had brought flowers to Cady and not to her? Where was Rich?

Hope smacked her lips and spun right off her chair. Even mad she looked so good, blond movie star good.

Lucas came back. "Can we scram?" he said to Cady.

"Will we see you at the cast party?" Cady asked Hope.

"I guess," Hope said. She grabbed her leather hobo bag and walked away without another word.

Lucas stared after her. "I can't believe her. . . ." he muttered.

"Yeah," Cady said. "I didn't know Hope would act that way . . . but you know sometimes she can be . . ."

"Rhymes with witch," Lucas said. He ran his fingers through his hair. A deep crease appeared between his eyebrows as he glanced up at the ceiling. "She acted like I didn't exist."

"She's just like that sometimes," Cady said, trying hard not to make excuses. "You know what I mean."

"I know," Lucas said through gritted teeth. "Believe me, I know."

Chapter Twenty-One

April 27, 2:14 PM
Hope

One of the ironies of being an upperclassman was that the older a student got, the more hideous the accommodations got. Hope couldn't stand the puke-green lockers reserved for Chesterfield seniors. And she hated the other kids who shared her locker bank even more.

There was this one girl who would always press up against Hope's locker bank with an iPod hanging from one ear, bobbing her head in time with the music, banging the locker with her free hand, and snapping at least three pieces of bubble gum at once. Hope despised the sticky pink-watermelon smell. All she wanted to do was thwack the girl on the back and make her swallow the gum in one dangerous gulp.

When the class bell finally rang, Hope didn't thwack anyone. She didn't even move. Calculus weighed on her conscience. Yesterday Mr. Guiney had embarrassed Hope by asking a question she didn't know how to answer, and today she hadn't finished the assignment. Who gave a crap about finishing math homework when there were only a few weeks of high school left?

As crowds of students rushed past the lockers and into the stairwell with a loud *whoosh*, Hope stood there facing the interior of her locker, pretending to look at her textbook or search for a notebook way in the back.

Before long, someone tugged on the sleeve of her yellow angora sweater. It was Lenora Less, one of Hope's friends from the Chesterfield party scene. They both liked to watch soccer matches and compare notes about the guys.

"Wanna cut with me, Hopie? Robert's on the security door downstairs and says he'll let us out of the building."

"I really can't, Lenora . . ." Hope said.

"Who says you can't? Come on! We can go get a manicure," Lenora replied. She dangled her Frosted Plum nail tips in front of Hope's face.

Hope shook her head. "Not me. I just had my nails done. And besides, I should go to calculus," she added with a thoughtful sigh.

"Since when do you care about class—especially *math*?" Lenora asked with a shudder. She made a sour lemon face. "You *have* to come. Pam's meeting us there after school's over. We could get a cappuccino."

"No, really, Lenora. I'm not leaving." Hope's voice was sharp this time.

"Look, Hopie, I know you're all into staying here and pretending to be straight edge . . ."

"*Look*, Lenora," Hope said firmly. She grabbed the strap on Lenora's little pink leather backpack. "Not leaving. Not now. Got it?"

Lenora rolled her eyes. "Got it. Take a Valium or something." Lenora calmly unclipped and reclipped the barrette in her brown hair, smoothed her hands against her jeans, and turned away. "See you."

"If I feel like it," Hope mumbled. Lenora was already halfway down the hall.

Hope looked inside her locker again. Something was stuck at the bottom, in the back, that she hadn't noticed before. It looked like a photograph, caught between the locker's edge and Hope's binder for English. As she pulled it out, the edge tore.

Staring back at Hope from the photo were she and Cady, both of them dressed up for the first act of *The Children's Hour*. The stage manager had taken photos of the cast in costume. Hope had pulled this one off the wall.

"There you are."

Hope spun around.

"I saw you with those guys," Lucas said calmly. He wore loose black shorts and his soccer team shirt. "First time was in the auditorium a few weeks back. I saw you again in the parking lot," he said again.

"Lucas." Hope said his name with a hiss. She stepped back. "Don't do this."

"Who were those jerk-offs?"

"What do you care?"

"Are you screwing both of them, too?"

"You're sick. Get away from me," Hope said sharply. "You're scaring me, Lucas. Quit terrorizing me."

"*Terrorizing?*" Lucas repeated incredulously. "How dramatic. How typical."

"Typical?" Hope said, rolling her eyes. "Leave me alone, Lucas. Get a beer and drown your sorrows somewhere else."

"What are you talking about?" Lucas asked.

"My parents always say the apple doesn't fall too far from the tree. I guess that's true for you."

Lucas's jaw dropped. "What's *that* supposed to mean?"

"Give it up, Lucas. I know all about your father and you're probably just like him." Hope took a breath. She could see Lucas's eyes darting from side to side. He shot her a confused look.

"How? How do you know? What?" Lucas tried to talk but the words came out all jumbled.

"I know your father is a drunk," Hope snapped. She knew her words stung like needles. But Hope needed to use all the weapons at her disposal.

"I can't believe . . ." Lucas said quietly. "I never told you anything about my dad or his trouble with . . ."

"Information gets around," Hope said matter-of-factly.

She glanced over her shoulder to see if anyone was looking now. The nearest group of kids was way over by a set of doors down the hall. Hope lowered her voice to a whisper so no one would hear.

"Find someone else who will help you with your problems, Lucas. *Not* me."

"I can't believe this. I can't believe you," Lucas said. "Didn't our time together mean anything?"

"Our time together?" Hope repeated coolly. "Lucas, you'd better stop this now — or else."

"Or else *what*?" Lucas asked.

Hope saw his eyes flash with desperation this time. She countered with a hard stare.

"I saved those messages on my cell phone, you know," Hope said, her words still loaded with venom.

"What messages?" Lucas asked.

"You know what messages. Leave me alone." Hope pushed herself away from Lucas, but she was still wedged between where he stood and the locker.

"I don't want to have to call the police," Hope continued, trying as hard as she could to sound threatening while still keeping her voice down.

"Police?" Lucas let out a gasp. "Are you kidding me? This is between *us*, Hope."

"Not anymore. I'll tell them everything. *Everything.*"

Lucas threw his arms into the air and let out a loud exhale. He twitched nervously, still not defeated. Hope shifted from side to side. "I have to go," Hope blurted. But then Lucas extended his arm against the locker like a steel gate. He didn't want her to go anywhere.

"I'm still coming to see you in the play," Lucas said, cocking his head to the side.

"The play? You can't. I don't want you there."

"I'm going to the last show. Cady asked me."

Hope looked around. Why wasn't anyone walking by? Where *was* everyone? Where was Cady? She tried to wriggle free from the barrier he'd put up, but there was no way out. Lucas wouldn't budge.

"You know, I wrote another song for you," Lucas said, trying to make eye contact.

From the pit of her stomach, Hope felt a surge of strength. She pushed Lucas's arm away.

"You know what your problem is?" Hope yelled, glaring at Lucas. "Music. You think it can save the world. You think just because you want something to be true that makes it true. Well, you're wrong. Life isn't some stupid song."

Lucas's jaw slackened. He let out a little laugh, a nervous laugh.

"Hope, don't do this. I know what we need. What *you* need—"

"You don't know *anything*," Hope said, finally shoving him away once and for all. She slammed her locker shut. "You think because you finally came on my scene all mysterious, the new kid at this school—that you can act however you want? You think you get a million chances to have everyone like you and want you? Well, I don't want you. I never have."

Hope looked up and down the corridor. Someone must have overheard. She was talking so loud. But nobody stopped or stared. The only people Hope saw were a couple of kids rushing to class, and one teacher who poked his head out of a classroom door and then ducked back inside again.

"Consider yourself warned, Lucas. I mean it," Hope said firmly.

"You always say what you don't mean," Lucas said. He was still trying.

Hope didn't stick around to hear any more. Without another word, she hustled toward the stairwell and pushed through the swinging doors. Her heart rate increased; she could feel the tightness in her upper chest.

Lenora said the security guard downstairs would be waiting. Maybe Hope would send the guard back upstairs and scare Lucas.

At the very least, Hope would hook up with Lenora for that manicure. There was nothing like a little Green Tea Lemonade at the Twin Nails salon to make a girl feel like herself again. She needed time to regroup and figure out her next move.

Chapter Twenty

April 16, 5:15 PM
Cady

It was a warm, breezy night. From her perch on the back steps, Cady looked out over the school courtyard.

Last year, she'd signed up to help the Chesterfield garden club plant bulbs everywhere. Their hard work was beginning to show. Crocuses popped up around the edges of flower beds, and a little purple went a long way. Tulips would be coming soon with their reds and oranges and pinks, and then everyone would have to give in to the fever of spring.

While the drama club crew worked inside hanging lights, cast members of *The Children's Hour* hung outside with scripts in hand, running lines. It was going to be a long rehearsal tonight. Actors waited until they were called inside and directed to stand in designated places under spotlights. Cady always wondered why the director, Ms. Wagner, really needed the actors there, since they did nothing more than stand in spot A and then move to spot B about a hundred times. You didn't need any special talent to stand still on a piece of masking tape.

But here they were, trapped in drama purgatory.

Most kids thought it was fun to be at school at this time of day, and Cady knew they were right, on some level. It was like being a member of an exclusive after-hours club—especially on a night like tonight, when the air smelled like flowers and wet earth. But waiting around could get boring fast, even on a beautiful spring evening. Even in the company of Hope, who'd become Cady's brand-new after-hours friend.

Hope and Cady hadn't always been friends. Not by a long shot. In fact, they'd been enemies for years, circling in different cliques, passing each other in the halls without words. Hope was queen of the surly stare, and over the years Cady's face had been covered by invisible skid marks from Hope's many parting glances.

Seventh grade was when their whole mess began.

That was when Hope White called Cady Sanchez a boy-stealing bitch, even though Cady hadn't stolen anyone, ever. It was when Hope spread the rumor that Cady was a liar and a backstabber who could never be trusted. They were generic lies, but for whatever reason, everyone believed Hope.

And so began Cady's slow journey inside.

Inside wasn't all terrible or terrifying. There was the music. Cady wrote a song called "Eve and My Adam" and entered it into a national contest for teen songwriters. Much to her amazement, she won second prize for lyrics. The next two years, she won other prizes in other categories. As she learned other instruments, Cady made other arrangements, entered other contests. She took voice lessons. She pried herself half-open like a clamshell, maybe for the first time.

And so here they were, Cady and Hope, yin and yang, declared enemies now cast together, beating the heaviest of odds, not only to become friends again but to become good friends, with their onstage relationship bleeding over into real life, or at least into rehearsal life.

After running over her monologues and scenes a few times, a song began to brew in Cady's head. She wished she had brought her guitar along for the evening, so she could hide out in a corner of the courtyard, strumming chords. She'd play "Case of You" by Joni Mitchell, or other mellow tunes. Lately, Cady liked listening to Joni, Norah, Aimee, Joss, and Elliott Smith—even though his music made her very, very sad.

Inside the wide pocket of Cady's book bag was a large plastic sleeve stuffed with scraps of paper, and envelopes with notes written on the back. Songwriting was a constant wherever she went: at rehearsal, at home, in the park, even.

Music always got right to the core of whatever Cady was experiencing. She would listen to her favorite songs on Dad's old turntable, straining to hear over skips and scratchy background sounds the *plinks* and *strums* of instruments. She imagined herself playing music in some dark bar where everyone smelled like black coffee or clove cigarettes, and the warm, dreamy whispers of an audience belonging just to her.

"What are you doing?" Hope asked Cady, sitting beside her.

Cady shook her head, putting away a cluster of index cards. "Just writing."

Hope's cell phone beeped. She glanced down at the display and then shoved it deep into her bag.

"What are you writing?" Hope asked, distracted.

Her phone beeped again.

"Don't you need to answer that?" Cady asked.

Hope shook her head even though the phone kept right on beeping. "I should just turn it off," she said with a huff, taking it back out of the bag. She glanced down at the display again and let out a big sigh.

"Is something wrong?" Cady asked.

"No. Well. It's that guy. The one I told you about. He keeps paging me. I asked him not to call me here. He *knows* I have play rehearsal tonight."

Hope held up her cell. Cady saw the readout.

RUNN4U

"Who is he?" Cady asked, genuinely concerned.

"Just this guy . . . who . . . won't leave me alone. . . ."

"Hope, are you shaking?" Cady asked. She put her arm around Hope's shoulder.

"Of course I'm not shaking. It's just cold out here," Hope snapped. She stood up and walked away.

Cady tried not to react, but she couldn't help feeling a little hurt by Hope's flip response. She watched as Hope walked over to Rich, one of the stage managers, who was chilling outside with a cigarette. Hope grabbed Rich by his studded belt. With one hand, she twirled her hair between her fingers, and with the other hand she touched Rich's shoulder as she talked. Rich wasn't saying much.

It wasn't the first time Cady had seen them together.

Cady had seen Hope and Rich fooling around one time, outside the local movieplex and another time backstage before rehearsal. Whenever Cady asked Hope about it, Hope made Cady promise not to mention it, like she was a little embarrassed.

She didn't look embarrassed now.

It was nearly ten o'clock by the time rehearsal ended. Parents arrived to pick up freshmen in the play. Seniors, juniors, and sophomores headed for home alone.

"Want to walk out to the bus together?" Cady asked Hope as they headed away from the school. "I'm taking the M411."

Hope shook her head. "Oh no . . . Sorry . . . Can't."

She pulled out her cell phone.

"Daddy? Hi!" Hope spoke loudly into the receiver. Cady listened as Hope told her father that rehearsal was running really, *really* late. She asked him to meet her in front of the school after eleven.

"Eleven?" Cady asked after Hope clicked off her cell. "Hope, it's only ten."

"I know that," Hope said with a sly smile. She shoved the phone into her jacket.

Cady needed to invest in a cell phone, like Hope. She was probably the only kid in class who didn't have one.

"Well, I guess I'll see you tomorrow," Cady said.

"Yeah," Hope answered, pressing buttons, distracted. "Tomorrow . . . sure . . ."

Cady lugged her bag and guitar case for two blocks to catch the bus. The slow grind of tires rolling up and down the street had a steady beat that got Cady thinking about music again. If she didn't have so many bags to juggle, she would have pulled out her notebook or the index cards to write a little. Cady had learned that eavesdropping was the best way to cheat at lyric writing. Why invent words when you could just copy something that a stranger said or did? Cady's guitar teacher once told her that muses like to hide. She had to nab a lyric wherever she could find one.

Besides, there was so much to write about out here on Center Street: a stray cat in the middle of the boulevard; a man lugging plastic shopping bags filled with clothes; another man with his tie loosened, toting a briefcase; a woman dressed up in sequins with nowhere to go. Standing there at the bus stop, Cady gazed up at the bubble of a white moon, three-quarters full. The moonlight cast a silver glow on the pavement. Across the street, two other figures in the darkness laughed, chasing each other. Their voices echoed, and Cady strained to listen.

"Stop it. No, I really mean it!" the girl cried. "You'll get me in trouble!" Cady recognized Hope's voice right away. Hope ran away but then let herself get caught again. Rich, the stage manager, was by her side.

Cady watched as they slipped into a municipal lot at the side of the road and got into the backseat of a car — his car? — together.

Just then the M411 screeched its brakes and pulled into the bus stop, blocking Cady's view.

"You getting on?" the bus driver croaked at her.

Cady quickly grabbed her stuff and boarded the bus. She scrambled toward a seat so she could see more of Hope and Rich. But the bus pulled out too fast.

Disappointed, Cady grabbed a cold metal handle and steadied herself into one of the single seats. Outside the bus window, she gazed at shadows, neon lights, and the passing glint of fenders and glass. She heard the screech of wet brakes and the faraway wail of a siren and wondered about Hope and Rich and whatever they were doing in the back of the car. Then she closed her eyes and tried to think of a song to make her forget.

Music surged inside Cady's head. She heard a piano. And then a flute. It was the start of a low, sweet love song. Unfortunately, it wasn't *her* love song. By the time the bus stopped at her corner, all the music inside Cady's head had played itself out.

And everything inside Cady turned to silence.

Chapter Nineteen

April 15, 1:29 PM
Cady

"Lucas . . . um . . . can I ask you something?"

Lucas rubbed his eyes with his knuckles and squinted at Cady.

"Ask me something?" he mumbled.

He slouched at a remote table at the back of the school library with at least ten hardcover books opened in front of him. Cady recognized a few of the titles: *The Da Vinci Code*; Dante's *Inferno*; *The Amazing Adventures of Kavalier & Clay*. Lucas was always reading something, but he never finished anything. He'd quickly browse through chapters One or Two of one novel, and then move quickly on to the next book.

"So, tell me. How can you skim-read *that*?" Cady asked, pointing to the fat, bedraggled copy of the *Inferno*. She let out a low, knowing laugh, but Lucas looked annoyed. He shoved his flattened palm in between the pages where he'd stopped.

"What did you say?"

"Don't be a grouch," Cady said. She took the seat across from him. "I wanted to talk — just for a minute."

"Minute's up," Lucas said. He gestured at his pile. "I'm a little busy, as you can see."

"Busy pretending to read?" Cady cracked.

Now Lucas had to smile. He reached out and rested his hand on Cady's arm.

"All right," he said. "Just keep it low. Marian the Librarian is in a pissy mood today."

Dappled light fell across the table, across the pages of another open book. Cady looked away and swept a strand of her brown hair off her face. She pulled the rest of her hair into a large tortoise clip atop her head.

Ever since the afternoon at Blue Notes music store, things between Cady and Lucas had shifted like tectonic plates. The friction between them was at least a six on the Richter scale. Cady worried about aftershocks.

"Hear from any colleges?" Cady asked.

Lucas shrugged. "Nah. I don't know if I'm going to Bentley Community, or State, and that's kinda bugging me out. I'm beginning to think I might not even get into my safety schools."

"I was talking to Hope the other day about schools, and she —"

"Hope?" Lucas furrowed his brow.

"Hope White."

"You're friends now?"

"Well, you know that for whatever reason, well, for good reasons, she and I have gotten closer lately. . . ."

"Closer? Get a room." Lucas smirked.

Cady bridled a little bit, but she wasn't sure why. Why had he said that?

"You know, Hope got early acceptance to Stanford," Cady said.

"So?" Lucas said. "Am I supposed to care?"

"Something she said, though—at rehearsal," Cady continued, "got me thinking, has me worried."

"What—did she run out of lip gloss or something?"

"Lucas, come on," Cady said. "I just think maybe she's in real trouble."

"Oh, please. Ms. Popular? Her life is perfect," Lucas said, tapping a pencil on the table.

"Nobody's life is perfect," Cady insisted.

"Except for mine," Lucas cracked.

"I'm serious, Lucas. Hope told me some guy is stalking her."

"What?" Lucas said, with real shock in his voice.

"I know. I can't believe it either."

"Why would she say that to you?" Lucas said, his face turning a little pale.

"I don't know. She trusts me."

Lucas sat up straighter. "So why tell me?"

"I thought maybe you might know who's doing it."

"Do I look like a cop or something?" Lucas asked, pushing up his sleeves.

"Noooo." Cady giggled. "I just thought—"

Cady stared at the soft hair on Lucas's wrist. Her fingers twitched with an impulse to reach and touch, but instead, she clasped her hands together in her own lap.

Cady had deliberately come to Lucas for hints about Hope's problem. Cady knew Lucas didn't have a lot of friends in their class, since he'd only been at the school since the start of the senior year. Even so, he always seemed to have an accurate read on people, as if he wore X-ray glasses every time.

"I was thinking that maybe," Cady continued, "maybe this guy . . . the stalker . . . maybe it's someone on the soccer team."

"The soccer team?" Lucas laughed, but it sounded strained. "You must be joking. What's his name?"

"Obviously, if I knew his name I wouldn't be asking you, would I?"

"What do Bebe and Marisol think?"

"They think Hope's lying. Of course. But Bebe hates Hope." Cady sighed. "What do *you* think about Hope, Lucas? Seriously. I trust your judgment."

"I think Bebe and Marisol are right. Hope lies like a rug." He laughed at his own lousy joke.

"But why would she make up something like this?" Cady asked.

"Trust me, I know her type," Lucas said. "I wouldn't be surprised if she secretly wanted the entire soccer team to stalk her — every last horn dog in cleats —"

"Lucas, that's gross," Cady said, blushing.

"Cady, let me ask you something," Lucas cut in, looking slightly annoyed. "Is this little Q & A session about Hope or is this about you? Are *you* the one who is in some kind of trouble? What's really going on here?"

Cady stared back at him. "I told you," she said.

Lucas scoffed. "You tell me a lot of things."

"This is NOT about me," Cady said firmly.

Lucas reached across the table and lightly placed his hand atop hers. Cady wanted to be angry but she went limp at his touch. The hair on Lucas's wrist *was* softer than it looked. She tried to read Lucas's face, as if his expression would clue her in to the way his mind was working right now. His lips were slightly parted, exposing a chipped front bottom tooth. She loved that tooth. She loved it as much as his scars.

"What kind of friend is Hope, Cady?" Lucas asked. "When we first met, you told me how twisted Hope was back in junior high. What makes you think she *isn't* twisted now?"

"Because people can change," Cady said.

Lucas snickered. "Yeah, they sure can."

"I want to believe in the good about people. Don't you?" Cady asked.

Lucas gulped. "Of course," he said, finally getting serious. "I didn't mean to imply —"

"I'm sorry I bothered you, Lucas," Cady interrupted. She pulled her arm away from his and looked over her shoulder. A stained-glass window along one wall of the library cast a purplish yellow hue on the smooth floor.

"You worry me lately," Lucas said.

"I worry *you?*" Cady replied. That wasn't what she wanted him to say.

She wanted Lucas to finger the collar of her shirt, pull her close, and talk about chords and love and crooked destiny like he'd done over the phone one night. He'd said so many things since New Year's that made her believe in him — and in the possibility of them. But now he sounded like he felt sorry for her.

"We done here?" Lucas said, abruptly, grabbing a book from his pile. "Because like I said, I need to work."

"Fine," Cady sighed. "I'll go."

Cady stood up, grabbed her bag, and started to walk away, but something invisible pulled her right back to the table, to Lucas. It was all the things she'd remembered. It wasn't him. It was *them*. Cady planted her hands on the table's edge and leaned in.

"What happened, Lucas?" Cady asked. "We used to be able to talk — to really talk about things that mattered."

Lucas looked away, but Cady mined her courage and kept talking. She spoke steady and slow.

"We used to write music together, Lucas. I miss finding words. With you. I miss our songs."

"Our songs?" Lucas looked up, scratching his head. "God, Cady, you're always missing something, someone. You're talking about Hope White as if she's your best friend? Come on. She isn't. You know that. And now you're analyzing *our* relationship and what's changed with us?"

"Right," Cady said in a low, controlled voice. She wanted to grab his face and kiss him and make him promise with his whole being that things could be good again between them. But Cady knew things between them were going backward, not forward.

"Why can't you just accept things the way they are?" Lucas asked.

Cady felt the tears but she swallowed — hard. She couldn't let the dam break. She couldn't let Lucas see. He hurt too much. As she stood there, speechless, Lucas stood up. The wide pile of books on the table collapsed in on itself, but Lucas didn't seem to care. He grabbed his backpack and left the mess behind.

"Where are you going?" Cady asked.

"I'm late," Lucas replied.

"Late for what?"

Lucas didn't answer. He started across the library carpet, and then through a pair of swinging red doors.

"Lucas, this is nuts," Cady said, struggling to catch up with him. "You're running away?"

"No, I'm not," Lucas said.

And then he disappeared around a corner.

Chapter Eighteen

April 8, 3:50 PM
Hope

Ms. Wagner pounded her fist on the long table in front of the stage.

"Do it again," she commanded. "You were supposed to know this scene last week, Miss White. Quit wasting our time."

Onstage, Hope shook her hands out from her side. The pressure of the upcoming first performance was beginning to seep into her consciousness — and her actions.

She wasn't ready. She had other things on her mind.

The auditorium was cooler than usual, but it was a wetter-than-average, early April day, the kind of damp day that got under a person's skin. It had been raining outside for almost a week and had only stopped this morning.

"April is the cruelest month," Ms. Wagner had said. Each evening, as she corralled everyone onstage for light cues and run-throughs, Ms. Wagner would act tough, but she'd use poetry to do it. She'd spout T. S. Eliot or William Shakespeare because she thought long-ago poets and playwrights could say things so much smarter than she could. As far as Hope was concerned, *anyone* was smarter than Fat Ass.

After Ms. Wagner had dismissed everyone from the rehearsal, Hope and Cady exited the hall together. When they were out of earshot of the other kids in the play, Hope stopped in mid-stride.

Cady looked worried. "Hope? Are you okay?"

Hope clutched at her chest and shook her head. "No," she whispered. She turned down a quiet hall and stepped into one of the restrooms. Cady followed.

"What happened?" Cady asked. "You were fine in rehearsal—"

All at once, Hope burst into tears, flapping her arms like a goose and turning on the faucet to splash water on her face.

"I hate this," Hope cried. "I hate all of this. You have no idea what's happening to me. . . ."

"In the play?"

"No, no." Hope shook her head. "In life."

"What? Tell me."

Hope looked right into the mirror and inhaled. But on the next exhale, no words came out. Just more tears.

"Hope, I'm here," Cady said, touching her friend's arm.

"It's cold in here, isn't it?" Hope asked. She leaned over her bag, pulled out a knit blue poncho, and tugged it over her shoulders.

Cady hopped up onto the graffiti-covered radiator under the bathroom window. "Sit down. Tell me what's going on," she offered.

Hope wasn't talking, and she wasn't sitting either. She paced across the bathroom floor. "I have a problem. No, a secret," Hope finally admitted.

Cady nodded. "Well, we all have secrets," she said. "Don't we?"

Hope stopped to lean over the sink. "Do we?" she asked the mirror. Then she turned back to Cady. "I've been acting."

Cady looked intrigued. "Well, duh," she said, obviously trying to lighten the mood a little. "We're in a play."

"You don't get it," Hope continued. "I mean I've been acting all the time. Onstage. Offstage. At home. At school. . . . I act like life is normal and things are normal, but . . ." Her voice trailed off.

"I don't understand," Cady said, nervous.

Hope picked up her bag. "I didn't think you would. Forget it. I hoped you would, but . . . we should go."

Cady was speechless. She hopped off the radiator and followed Hope back into the hallway. A cluster of boys barged through a set of doors and narrowly missed crashing into both girls. Their voices rebounded off the walls and lockers like the sharp pop of a dozen basketballs.

"Well, hello there, lay-deez," one boy said, staring at Cady and Hope as he walked by. "Mmm-mmm good."

As the boy turned, he tripped over his friend's sneaker and Cady started to giggle. The boys chased each other to another set of double doors farther down the hall.

"What a loser," Cady said, still laughing a little.

"Cady," Hope said, grabbing her arm. "Please don't. It isn't funny."

"What? I'm sorry. . . . I didn't . . ."

"How can you laugh?"

"I'm sorry. . . ."

Hope crossed her arms in front of her and rocked from

side to side. She sensed that Cady was about to hug her, when the cell phone in her purse buzzed.

Hope quickly juggled the phone, glancing at the caller ID. "It's him," Hope said. She clicked the phone off, her eyes wide.

"Him?"

"This guy," Hope said, wiping her nose with the tip of her sleeve. "Um . . . do you have a tissue?"

"I think so," Cady said. She reached into her bag for a package of Kleenex.

Hope blew her nose. She knew RUNN4U would call again, but when? She hoped it would be soon. Cady would be here as a witness.

"Hope, what's going on?" Cady asked cautiously.

Hope explained — slowly. She'd met a boy a few months earlier, near work, a boy with round, brown eyes like coasters. It was nothing, Hope said, really nothing. But then the boy got the wrong idea.

"I don't know why I'm telling you all this," Hope explained, sniffling.

"It's okay," Cady said. "Go ahead. I don't mind."

Quietly, they walked toward the lobby, side by side, in perfect step, ignoring the other students who passed.

"Does being friendly mean that you owe a person something? I mean, this guy actually said, 'I can read your mind,' like he wanted to control me or something," Hope went on. "Maybe he *could* read my mind, because I feel like I'm losing it."

She and Cady stopped walking. They'd reached the

main lobby. A few goth girls stood by the display cabinet along one wall. Cady recognized them from lunch as the members of a girl band called Enemy of the People.

"Hope, I'm so sorry about the boy. Can we talk more another time? My music teacher is waiting upstairs, and I just have to grab my guitar case in the music room."

"Oh," Hope said. "I can't believe I just unloaded on you like that. I'm sorry."

"No, no. *I'm* sorry. Hey, are you going to be okay?"

"Sure," Hope said, wiping her cheek with the back of her hand.

"Be careful, Hope," Cady said as she lifted her book bag to her shoulder and headed for the second floor.

Hope smiled. "Sure," she said again, her voice just a hush now.

After Cady left, Hope turned and headed in the opposite direction, toward the back exit that led into the school parking lot. Her Volkswagen convertible was waiting for the ride home. On the way out, Hope stopped back into the bathroom and frantically wiped her mottled face with a wet paper towel. The mascara Hope had applied that morning came off easily onto the paper in thick black lines. Carefully, she reapplied makeup, including the bright berry lip gloss that she'd stashed in one pocket of her purse.

So much work done, Hope thought as she puckered up at her reflection.

So much done and so much left to do.

Chapter Seventeen

April 2, 10:08 AM
Cady

For Lucas

A little piece of me
Caught

Cady looked up from the scrap of yellow, wrinkled paper that had been refolded and restuffed into a dozen different pockets on its way to becoming a real song. It bore the marks of a good scrap: torn edges, coffee cup rings, and doodles on the side.

A little piece of me
Caught

A few rows ahead in the auditorium, Cady spotted Hope White's blond French twist, held in place with a woven black leather barrette. Hope sat between two senior boys, wide-shouldered football players dressed in neat blue shirts. Cady had never noticed them before. They didn't exactly seem like Hope's type.

Then again, there were so many things about Hope that Cady didn't know.

She glanced back down at her song notes.

When you love me with your eyes
And close your arms around
You turn the sand into a pearl

A tune lilted in the back of Cady's head. If only the words would come together a little better and she could play it at Big Cup. She'd had a gig there back in mid-March, but the old songs that she'd already played a million times didn't feel right anymore.

The gray upholstered chair creaked as Cady leaned back and gazed at the ceiling, silently beckoning inspiration to strike.

"Excuse me, coming through," a boy said.

Cady's heart skipped. It was Lucas. She didn't want him to see the song. But when she glanced down at her lap, the scrap was gone. Her heart jumped.

"Hello, you," Lucas grunted, finally falling sideways into the seat. He slammed his one bad knee into the chair.

"Ouch," Cady said. "*That* hurt."

"What's this?" Lucas asked, touching Cady's knee. He held up the piece of paper. The scrap had been stuck—with static—to Cady's skirt. Cady snatched it back.

The swell of chatter in the auditorium continued to rise and dive, and Cady stayed afloat, ears and eyes open for the assembly announcements. She still had a clear view of Hope from here, and of everything Hope was doing. One of the muscle-heads at her side kept curling his arm around Hope's shoulder, and even leaned into her ear at one point. What was he whispering? Was that his tongue? Cady couldn't tell. She knew it didn't look innocent.

"Slut," Lucas said in a low voice. No one could hear him except for Cady, and she couldn't believe what she'd heard.

"What did you say?" Cady asked.

"Nothing," Lucas mumbled and ducked low in his seat. He pushed his head through his knees, the same position the airlines always ask a passenger to get into before the plane dives into the sea. Cady looked away, vaguely annoyed. What was his problem?

Four rows ahead, Hope White leaned away from the boy who had been nuzzling her. She turned 180 degrees and caught Cady's eye.

"Hey." Cady mouthed the word and waved.

Hope gave Cady a polite smile and then craned her neck like she was looking around the room for someone else. Then the guy on her left leaned into her ear again.

Lucas was still leaning forward. "What are you doing down there?" Cady asked, looking down.

She touched Lucas's blue oxford shirt, starchy in the shoulders. It smelled like dryer sheets.

Lucas raised his head and finally inched his body back up into the chair again. He acted relaxed about the whole scene, but Cady sensed the opposite was true. Lucas had his legs all stretched out like an easygoing cowboy in front of the campfire, but he kept scraping his shoes against the bottom of the chair in front of them. Nervous habits die hard.

At the auditorium podium, the principal, Mr. Herman, tapped the large microphone. Feedback shrieked like a stuck gull. Everyone covered their ears and moaned.

Cady loved moments like this, the cliché moments from every bad teen movie, with the cliché characters to boot. These were the people and places that fed her song-writer head. Mr. Herman had the characteristic toupee, handlebar mustache, thick metal-framed glasses, hairy knuckles, gray suit with pants one size too small, and gray teeth (or were they dentures?) to match. The only thing missing from his ensemble was the wad of toilet paper affixed to his left shoe.

"Attention, students," the principal said, tapping the mic. "We're having a special ad hoc prom committee meeting for seniors this morning. Please settle back into your seats so we can discuss your upcoming celebration."

Someone booed, and the student audience cracked up. Cady and Lucas laughed along with everyone else. Up ahead of them, Hope and her two boys laughed, too.

"Do you know those guys?" Cady whispered to Lucas. She pointed to the two boys sitting with Hope.

"Nope." Lucas shrugged. "Am I supposed to know?"

"Are they in our class or are they juniors?" Cady asked. "I don't recognize them."

"I don't know," Lucas repeated. "Who's the girl?"

"The girl?" Cady nudged Lucas with her elbow. "Come on. That's Hope White. You know that."

"Oh? Yeah, I guess so. . . ."

Cady made a face. How could Lucas say he didn't recognize Hope when *every* guy in their class had memorized and categorized Hope's every inch? Cady laughed to herself. This was proof once again that Lucas could be a space case. He hardly noticed his own classmates.

"Hello, everyone," Mrs. Foster, the home and careers

teacher, said into the microphone. Her voice was breathy, slow. The mood in the room shifted.

The committee of teachers and students responsible for organizing prom had decided not to designate a specific theme. No one liked circus or carnival or "Under the Deep Azure Sea." Instead of purchasing plastic decorations or a bubble machine, money for prom would be spent on a great DJ and location. They'd reserved DJ Beat, a guy who played in all the big clubs in New York, who just happened to be a cousin of one of the graduating seniors. The top ballroom pick was the Chesterfield Suites.

"Of course there will be no drinking, no funny business," said Mrs. Foster, sounding like a regular fuddy-duddy.

Cady faded in and out of the prom speech. She wanted to listen, but a part of her kept shutting off. Secretly, Cady had been looking forward to this event all of her years in high school. But she was spending more mental energy right now on someone else: Lucas. She stared at his empty hands and wished they were on her knee again. She wanted to bury her face in his shoulder and smell that shirt.

Smells like his lived in her memory like hot coals.

In front of them, one of the boys next to Hope pushed her elbow off the armrest of the chair. Hope laughed and turned to the boy with her eyes opened wide. Teeth gleamed. Hair shone. The boy leaned in like he was going to kiss her.

"Not so fast!" Hope appeared to say. She drew back but then touched the boy's face.

Cady looked on in a kind of awe. How did Hope manage to pull guys in but push them back at the same time?

Lucas moved and knocked his knee into the chair in front — again.

"Shit," he muttered.

"You okay?" Cady asked Lucas.

Lucas snapped his neck to the side and it cracked. "Never better," he said.

Cady settled back in her own seat. She was watching the back of Hope's head again, not the principal onstage.

All at once, Lucas threw his arm around Cady's shoulder.

"Lucas?" Cady was surprised by the gesture.

Lucas squeezed tight.

"Lucas?" Cady said his name again. His fingers pinched, but she liked the closeness. He'd never shown her affection in public. Not like this.

Cady wanted to say, "What's going on?" but she didn't say anything. Her face flushed, like watercolor paint on paper. She thought about the afternoon they'd played music together the week before.

"Is there something you want to ask me?" Cady said.

"Like what?" Lucas mumbled, his arm still around her.

"I don't know," Cady said. "Anything at all?"

Lucas shook his head.

"Seriously, Lucas," Cady prodded again. "Is there something you need to tell me?"

"Cady," Lucas replied deliberately. "Am I missing something?"

Cady sat back and nodded.

But she didn't say another word.

Chapter Sixteen

March 28, 3:11 PM
Cady

The front door at Lucas Wheeler's house was carved, worm-eaten wood with a small, beveled glass square at the top. Outside the door stood two stone pots, chipped and overgrown with weeds and dead ivy. The brass doorknob was loose and dull with the grime of many hands. The welcome mat had been rubbed bare, too, with comings and goings over the years.

Cady rang the doorbell and heard a dim buzzing sound. It was broken. Mr. Wheeler, Lucas's father, always insisted he was getting the place fixed up, but nothing ever seemed to improve.

They wouldn't have mattered much, these small house-keeping details, if Lucas Wheeler's family hadn't been so rich. Lucas didn't brag about his family finances, but everyone knew the truth. His great-grandfather had invented shoelace widgets, or rubber drain stoppers, or something like that. Lucas's dad, a retired Navy colonel, shared his portion of the wealth with seven siblings and their children and their children after that, so the inheritance was watered down a bit. But at the end of the day, it was still a fair bundle. So Lucas dressed in ratty jeans, but carried the best flip-up Nokia and drove a BMW convertible.

Cady didn't even have a car, unless she counted her loaner — Mom's Honda Civic with one taillight busted in the back.

As Cady punched the doorbell again, she heard it make a low, sick moaning sound. There would be only a few more buzzes left before the bell died completely.

A kid answered the door, a seventh grader maybe, with a mop of carrot-orange hair.

"Hey, what's up?" the boy chirped.

Cady fumbled with her guitar case. "Is Lucas home?"

"You selling guitars?" the kid asked.

All at once, Lucas appeared wearing running pants and a torn T-shirt that said BB10K. Cady had seen the shirt before. Lucas had run in a race called Bolder Boulder in Colorado the year before, on a trip with his dad.

"This is Linus," Lucas said, resting his hand on the scruffy side of the kid's neck. "My cousin. He's here with my aunt Rita."

Although she'd never met Aunt Rita or her son, Cady knew about them from Lucas. Ever since Lucas's mother, Abby, had been killed by a drunk driver two years before, Rita had taken on the "mom" role. She checked in on Lucas and his dad at regular intervals, which was easy because she only lived one town over.

"Glad to meet you, Linus," Cady said, extending her hand.

"No Charlie Brown cracks, got it?" Linus snapped, shaking Cady's hand as hard as he possibly could.

Cady pulled her arm back with a twinge. "Some grip," she said, shaking her hand out.

"He hangs on to everything a little too much," Lucas said.

Cady stepped into the entryway and dumped her coat on the staircase banister. Lucas carried her guitar case inside as Linus disappeared inside the house.

"I'm down in the basement," Lucas said. "You want to practice down there or outside? It's a little chilly, I thought. It's supposed to rain."

"Anywhere is fine," Cady said. "Basement's good."

She had only been to Lucas's house a few times before now, mostly to pick him up so they could go somewhere else. And she'd never been to his basement before. Hoping to get together a new repertoire for Big Cup, she had asked for his help with a few of her songs, and he'd said that his place was probably the easiest place to meet.

"Watch the stairs," Lucas said as he pointed the way down. "I'll grab a few drinks. What do you want?"

"Coke's fine," Cady said. "Or water. Whatever."

"Meet you down there," Lucas said. "And you don't have to worry about Boo Radley. Dad took him to the vet today."

Boo was Lucas's German shepherd mix, a dog that had outlived Lucas's own mother. Cady had met Boo a few times in Davidson Park, to play fetch or Frisbee.

The basement air was musty, and it got mustier on the way down. At the bottom of the staircase, Cady saw the source of the smell: litter boxes. There were four of them against a wall. One of them actually had a cat in it. Cady made a slight mewing noise, and the orange tabby flipped its tail into the air and pounced away.

The basement was like most other basements: rough

stone walls, washer and dryer in a separate area, worn carpets, old sofa, and the giant TV set with its veins of life, the electrical cords, attached to every X-Box/ Nintendo/PlayStation game console a person could imagine.

Cady heard the floorboards creak upstairs and briefly hoped Lucas would bring the Coke and not the water. She needed a jolt right about now. Cady's nerves were starting to tingle. She'd been thinking about Lucas a lot more, and being here inside his private space got her heart racing. She knew this was where Lucas wrote a lot of his music.

Cady pictured him on the sofa, playing a few chords. A Yamaha keyboard sat on a table not too far away.

I wrote a song for you, Cady, Lucas would say. At least that's what he would say in her dreams.

Oversized French movie posters for both Quentin Tarantino's *Kill Bill* and *Reservoir Dogs* caught Cady's attention. They hung unframed on the wall next to a triptych of photographs someone had taken of Lucas.

The photographs attracted Cady's gaze like magnets. One of the black-and-white photos showed the back of Lucas's head, blurry, at an angle, as he ran away. The next showed him holding up his hand so the person wouldn't take his picture. The third and last one showed half of Lucas's face, smiling at the photographer.

In the background of all three photographs Cady recognized The Woods, a park and residential complex on the other side of town. She'd only been there one especially windy day to fly a kite. But that was when she was little, before developers moved in with bulldozers and boxy apartment buildings.

98

Cady knew that some kids from school liked to go to The Woods to hook up. She stared at the three photographs of Lucas and imagined what it would be like to be there, alone, in the leaves, under the trees, with him.

"Beverages are served," Lucas said.

Cady caught her breath and turned quickly. "I didn't hear you coming back down," she said. "I was just . . ."

"Poking around," Lucas joked.

"Is that a photograph of your mom?" Cady asked, diverting her attention to another picture in a green-stained wood frame. It was a close-up of a woman's smiling face, taken near the ocean. Sunbathers and swimmers were visible in the background.

"That's her," Lucas said, staring at the picture.

"Pretty," Cady said.

Lucas reached out and brushed his fingertips along the top of the frame. "Yeah," he said.

"What happened to the frame? Is the glass cracked?"

Lucas made a face. "I meant to fix that. I'll get to it one of these days. I have to fix that mirror over there, too."

He pointed across the room to a small, frosted mirror with a corner missing.

"But broken mirrors are bad luck." Cady grimaced.

"Yeah, I know. But you know what else? Sometimes I think anything can be bad luck. And that same thing could just as easily be good luck, right? It's all just luck."

Just then, one of his other cats, a fat, black-and-white fluffy one, saw Lucas and purred. She rubbed in and out of his legs.

"Hello, Oreo," Lucas said.

Cady smiled at the name. She took her drink from Lucas and sat down on one section of the curved sofa with its flattened cushions.

"I've been working on a little riff," Lucas said, grabbing his own guitar. He took the pick and worked over the strings.

Cady listened intently, watching his fingertips go up and down the frets with smooth motions. She had an idea about playing a duet with him, maybe at Big Cup, but didn't dare ask. Lucas always told Cady she should be in the spotlight, not him.

"That's good," Cady said. He played it again and she smiled. "Sort of like Dashboard Confessional, right?"

"Yeah," Lucas said, taking a sip of his Coke. "I love that song 'Screaming Infidelities.' You heard their new one? What are you listening to these days?"

Cady shrugged. "Oh, I don't know. Death metal's cool."

Lucas cracked up so hard that the Coke spit out of his mouth. "Oh, so you're into the Dark Lord, huh?" he asked teasingly.

Cady rolled her eyes. "Yes, that's me, all over."

Lucas turned back to his guitar and broke into the opening bars from the Rolling Stones's "Gimme Shelter."

"I love that song," Cady said.

"I knew it. And I bet you're like all the girls who like the woman soloist backing up Mick on the original," he said. "I remember one time when . . ." Lucas stopped himself mid-sentence. "Aw, forget it. There was this one girl but she had no taste in music. She ruined songs for me. She ruined everything. . . ."

"Who?" Cady asked, too curious. She'd assumed Lucas had had girlfriends before he came to Chesterfield and perhaps even during the school year, but Lucas had never mentioned anyone special before now, not in all the times they had talked about school or music or running away to join the circus.

"Who ruined your songs?" Cady asked again.

"No one," Lucas snapped. "Forget it. Ancient, ancient history."

"Okay." Cady fell back into the sofa. "I'm sorry I asked."

"No, I'm sorry. Look, I'm still dealing with . . . this breakup . . . at least I think it's a breakup . . . I can't really talk about it." Lucas reached over and touched Cady. He moved his fingers up and down lightly on her forearm. "But I'm glad you came over," he added. "Really."

"That tickles," Cady said. Her breath was shallow.

Lucas was this close.

"So what music are you listening to again?" he asked, pulling away abruptly. "You didn't really answer me before."

"You know what I like." Cady nodded, the butterflies still dancing inside her. She wasn't even sure what she was saying, but she kept right on talking. "But these days Dad's been playing a lot of salsa. He's taking these dance lessons with my mom. And I like Bob Dylan lately, especially his old stuff. My mom has all his albums, and their hi-fi still works so I've been searching through their record collection."

"That's cool," Lucas said, smiling. "My dad has an old

Hank Williams LP somewhere. He mostly listens to talk radio, though." He looked away for a second and Cady grabbed the couch nervously.

"I think I've learned more about music from digging around in my parents' stuff," Cady said. "I guess I'm lucky they had such eclectic taste. You know, you're welcome to come over and go through all the stuff, too. The songs really inspire me to write. . . . But I guess you don't need some dusty record collection to help, since you can download almost anything off the Internet—"

Cady stopped mid-sentence.

"Am I talking too much?" she asked.

"Nah," Lucas said. "You make a hell of a lot more sense than most girls in our class, that's for sure. You get it."

Cady nodded. *I do get it*, she wanted to say, taking him into her arms. Sometimes talk was the best kind of foreplay. "You sign up for those drum lessons yet?" Cady asked, inching a little closer.

"Not yet," Lucas said.

"You know, I bet you could play any instrument you want to play."

Cady was, of course, thinking of herself.

"Well, before I do anything, I'll have to consult with my Buddha," Lucas said, pointing to a shelf across the room.

Cady stood up and walked over. "Him?" she asked, picking up a plastic green Buddha.

Lucas nodded. "I picked him up in a thrift shop down on Myrtle Street. Only two bucks and he glows in the dark. I know it's weird. But he's my inspiration these days."

Cady smiled. "It's not weird. Not really."

"Aren't you going to play me something you've been working on?" Lucas asked. He strummed a few chords.

When Cady picked up her guitar, he stopped. But when she played a chorus from a Rachael Yamagata tune, he joined in.

As music swirled around them, Cady's fingertips moved like magic up and down the guitar. Everything about this moment seemed magical.

"Good song," Lucas said, as they finished up. He propped his guitar up against the sofa and moved a little closer to where Cady sat. One of his knees was practically touching hers.

"What about playing one of *your* songs?" Lucas asked, pressing his knee against hers a little harder.

All at once, Cady felt a painful shyness take over, as if playing Lucas her new songs would be like peeling away parts of her soul. She wasn't very good at peeling.

"Looooook Ass!" Linus shouted from the top of the stairs.

Lucas chuckled. "Yes, worm," he called back.

"Mom's back and she needs your help!" Linus yelled. "NOW!"

Lucas moved his guitar to the side and stood up. "Sorry," he said to Cady. "I probably should go see what Aunt Rita wants."

"Of course," Cady said. "Do you need some help? I can come, too."

"No, no, it's cool."

Cady felt a flush of relief. She wanted to shout up the stairs, "Thanks, Linus!" since he'd come to her emotional rescue. *Emotional rescue.* That would have made a great song if the Rolling Stones hadn't already done it.

As Lucas walked away, he ran his hand over Cady's back, and she felt herself swoon. If only there weren't so many mixed signals. Lucas seemed ready to pounce and retreat at the same time. But no matter what had happened between them before, it was never clear what might happen today, right now, this very minute. With Lucas, why was a touch never really *the* touch?

Maybe it's that other girl, Cady thought. *The one who ruined songs.* Who *was* she and when had Lucas been seeing her? Was it before or after he and Cady had sort of gotten together?

She couldn't do the math inside her head.

Lucas bounded back down the basement steps.

"So Aunt Rita told me to get lost," Lucas said with a grin. "She knows what's up."

"She knows I'm here?" Cady asked.

Lucas plopped down on the sofa, practically onto Cady's lap.

"She knows *everything*," Lucas said. He stroked the top of Cady's knee like he was drawing figure eights.

Cady froze. She watched Lucas's finger and counted to herself.

One one-hundred, two one-hundred, three one-hundred.

Lucas reached up and ran his fingertip over her lip. Then he began to unbutton his own shirt — slowly. Cady's body quivered as she watched.

"Are you okay?" Lucas asked.

"I think so . . ." Cady said. "I mean, what are you — ? What are we — ?"

Slowly, Lucas lifted Cady's hands and pressed them onto his bare chest. His skin was so warm. His breath was slow and steady. She'd never wanted a kiss more than she wanted one right now.

And there it was: the touch that really *was* the touch. One kiss. And then another. They kissed again and again — longer than they had the one time before. Lucas's unshaven cheeks were rough but that didn't matter. Nothing mattered except the part where Cady felt his tongue and she thought she would stop breathing.

But then Lucas pulled back.

"Cat!"

From across the room, one of Lucas's nomadic cats scooted across the top of the sofa and leaped onto the rug. It sat down and flicked its tail around. This one had green eyes and pale yellow fur. It looked upset.

"That's Cat," Lucas said. "She never comes out to play. You should feel honored."

"Cat?"

"Yeah. I was pretty uninspired when I named her."

Cady had to laugh, even though she secretly wanted to throw the cat out the window for interrupting their perfect kiss. Somehow the moment between them had passed. Lucas buttoned his shirt again. He and Cady sat in silence for another few seconds, both petting the same cat.

"So, Cady . . . what's the deal with prom? Do you have a date yet?"

"A date?" Cady looked down. "You know I don't. What about you?"

Lucas shrugged off the question. "Not really."

He leaned over and pressed a strand of Cady's hair behind her ear.

"Maybe you and I should just go together," he suggested.

Cady gulped. She'd been hoping to hear that from Lucas for weeks. But his actual words made her reel. Did he mean it? Lucas veered between flirting and friendship so often that Cady had lost the ability to distinguish the two.

"Think of all the fun we'll have hanging on the sidelines and making fun of the band and all the bad outfits and the jocks dancing like the Tin Man," Lucas said.

Cady's brain synapses electrified with a flurry of important and useless words. They sped toward her tongue all at once, but she kept her mouth shut so all the words stayed inside. *Don't say the wrong thing or he'll take it back*, Cady told herself.

"Whoa. You got quiet all of a sudden. Did I say something wrong?" Lucas asked.

"No, no," Cady said.

She stroked the cuff of his flannel shirt.

"For once, Lucas Wheeler, you said everything right."

Chapter Fifteen

March 20, 7:12 PM
Lucas

Paddy's Diner had a burger deluxe special today, and Lucas ordered himself a plate with fries and extra tomato.

He'd been waiting too long already. As the waiter poured the sixth glass of water, Lucas rubbed the top of his boot under the booth seat ahead of him. He had the habit of shaking his leg or knee or moving his feet across the floor when he felt anxious about something — or someone. It wasn't really a habit that annoyed anyone in particular, but it quickly wore out the tops of his shoes, boots, and sneakers.

The round bells above the entrance door to Paddy's shook again with their *jangle-jangle* that made everyone in the place turn around. Lucas's head shot up for the hundredth time. He watched (truthfully, everyone in the place watched) a blond girl enter the diner. She was wearing a slim-fitting blue turtleneck sweater with golden thread woven into it, tight jeans, and a chain-link belt. Her brown boots had thin heels like twigs holding her up. Most girls Lucas knew could never walk in those sorts of shoes without teetering and tottering and eventually falling flat; but not this girl.

"Hey," Lucas said to Hope, his voice lilting.

"Let's get this straight. I'm only here because you begged."

Someone dropped a saucer behind the counter. The loud crash made everyone jump. A baby in another booth began to wail, and then the place quieted back down again.

Paddy's Diner was located far, far away from Chesterfield High, on the border of the neighboring town Lakemont. Paddy wasn't actually a person; he was a parrot who perched in a cage behind the counter. The bird never talked and was missing at least half of his tail feathers, but the owner kept him anyway.

Lucas had come here a lot when he first moved to Chesterfield. He would sit alone in a booth for hours, staring at Paddy's cage, or the BLOTTO video gambling monitor, or the enormous fish tank set up by the diner's front door. Inside the tank, hidden barbs and tetras darted in and out of the murky fake seaweed, in and out of darkness.

At this diner, Lucas felt the same way as those fish: half-visible. He never saw people he knew from school here. He never saw anyone he knew. It was what made it such a good place to meet Hope. Paddy's was a good place for secrets.

Lucas reached across the table for Hope's hand, the one with the ring. "How are you?" he asked.

Hope yanked her hand back. "Fine."

"You know, I've been working on a new song," Lucas said.

"Oh, like that's a surprise," Hope said, rolling her eyes. She looked across the diner and motioned for the waiter. He rushed to another table with five plates stacked across his shoulder and arm.

"Could I get a Diet Coke with two lemons, please?"

Hope barked when the waiter came back into view. It was the drink she always ordered.

The waiter nodded as he passed. "Of course," he said.

"I can't believe you wanted to come back *here*," Hope said.

"We always come here," Lucas said.

"*Came* here."

Hope opened up her bag, a small orange clutch with zippered pockets. She fished around and pulled out a pair of sunglasses with wide lenses.

"Too bright in here or what?" Lucas kidded.

"No, I'm looking for something," Hope said. She pulled out a small cloth bag with a drawstring and handed Lucas a turquoise charm necklace with a teeny bear claw strung on a thin black cord.

Lucas fingered the stone. "But I gave this to you."

"And I don't want it. The last thing I need is a reminder."

Lucas took a long, loud slurp from his half-drunk milk shake.

"God, can't you sip like a normal person?" Hope said. She crossed her arms and pulled them into her chest like she was bound into some kind of straightjacket.

The waiter brought over her Diet Coke, and the ice cubes clinked as Hope raised the glass for a drink. Liquid moved down her throat in four clear gulps. Her neck was clean and smooth, and Lucas could just barely see the line where she'd applied foundation to her face.

Lucas remembered all the times he had kissed and nibbled that neck. Hope tasted like a mixture of talcum powder and soap-scrubbed skin. Her neck was ready-made for a Dracula close-up: perfect shape, perfect texture, perfect, perfect, perfect.

Lucas glanced at his burger. He lifted it up to his mouth and took a bite. The juice ran down his chin.

"That's just gross," Hope said. "God. I don't know *why* I came here."

"Everything I do seems to gross you out these days, doesn't it?" Lucas said. He wiped his mouth with a napkin.

Hope leaned into the table. "You repulse me, Lucas."

"Repulse you?" Lucas coughed. "Gee, thanks."

He ran his hand across the edge of the table, imagining the blood beneath his skin, pumping through his body, into his heart.

There was no right way to feel about this moment.

"This was such a mistake," Hope said. She stared away from the table, over at the fish tank. "It's embarrassing."

"For who?" Lucas asked self-consciously.

"You have to stop calling, Lucas. You have to stop text-messaging me."

The waiter came by to refill their water glasses, and silence fell over the table. Lucas tapped his fingers on the table to a song beat. He needed all his courage.

"You know, prom's coming up," Lucas blurted.

"Prom?" Hope said the word like it was in Japanese or Farsi or some other language she didn't understand.

"Yeah, prom," Lucas said, grabbing the table. "Last week at the beach when we talked about going, we said——"

"We said what?" Hope asked incredulously.

"When we said we would tell everyone about us," Lucas said.

Hope laughed out loud. Lucas felt a current surge through his body. "Please, *please* don't do this, Hope," he said, trying hard to keep his voice down.

"Do what?" Hope said. "Lucas, I told you. The day at the beach was the last time. We're done."

Hope slid sideways down the booth and started to rise.

"Hope, where are you going? Don't—" Lucas lowered his voice. "I don't want to be angry. I'm sorry about before. I'm sorry. I'm sorry. Please, please stay. You have to stay."

Hope looked into his pleading eyes. She sank back into the booth.

"This is so pathetic," she said. "You know—"

"I know," Lucas said. "I said I'm sorry."

Hope's hands were on the top of the table again. Lucas grabbed for them. "We can't stop. I need you," he said.

"Lucas," Hope said firmly. She pulled her hands back. "You need to understand how I really feel. I feel—"

"I *know* how you feel." Hope's voice descended to a defiant whisper. "God. I never should have come here."

Without another word, Hope stood up, picked up her bag, and walked out the front door of Paddy's. No teetering. No tottering. No looking back.

Lucas felt a sharp tug in his pelvis and then in his shoulder. It quickly turned into shooting pain all over, a gush of nausea. Was this what it felt like to get flattened by a train?

"Check?" the waiter asked.

Lucas reached into his pocket and pulled out a wad of bills. Slowly, dazed, Lucas stumbled for the exit. He had a doctor's appointment today, but he was already late.

What was the point?

On the way out of Paddy's, Lucas glanced up at the bulletin board inside the front doorway. The board was crammed with flyers and postcards advertising housecleaners, nannies, and plumbers. It was beyond messy.

In one corner of the board, Lucas glimpsed something that looked familiar. Tacked in the left corner was a deeppurple flyer with the words BIG CUP PRESENTS at the top. Lucas scanned the page. The words were right there.

CADY SANCHEZ, FRIDAY, MARCH 19.

Lucas yanked down the flyer and stared at Cady's name. Then he crumpled it up and shoved it into his pocket before lurching back into the real world.

Chapter Fourteen

March 19, 8:23 PM
Cady

Some kid wearing a black beret, turtleneck, and stone-washed jeans shredded at the thighs stepped up to the microphone at Big Cup. He slid up the mic so it was the right height.

"Evening, people," his voice crackled. Someone at the controls adjusted the sound level, and the kid repeated himself. "Evening. Evening."

A steady clang of saucers and coffee mugs was like the rowdy overture to a night of mellow (and mostly guitar) music at the Chesterfield teen spot, Big Cup. Half the tables were filled with high-schoolers and college kids, although a few other, older local residents had come, too. Each table had a candle on top, so the room appeared to flicker with muted light.

In the evenings, the space was used for coffee and music. During the daytime it was a lunch restaurant for the downtown business crowd. At all times, the room served as makeshift gallery. The walls of Big Cup were covered with artwork — photographs, oil paintings, and even collage. Most of the art was for sale, although no one did much buying here at night. The only things most students could afford were coffee drinks and the occasional cover charge.

Cady stood by one of the far gallery walls, a thick slab of stone that was cold to the touch. She surveyed the crowd before heading backstage to her guitar and her place on the evening's set. She was scheduled third after Cassandra Told Me, a sister folk duo from the high school in the next town, and Harry Bell, a local guitarist/college student who worked part-time with Cady over at the Crestwood Music Center. Cady Sanchez was a familiar singer at Big Cup, but tonight was the first night she'd gotten top billing. In anticipation of the big event, Cady, with the help of Bebe and Marisol, had plastered purple flyers all over Chesterfield to drum up attendance.

Of course, there were familiar faces in the crowd. Marisol brought Ed, who she was calling her new "*tamale caliente.*" Bebe showed up with longtime boyfriend, Tony, in tow. And Cady's dad, Fernando, and brother, Diego, had made a special appearance tonight. They sat against a back wall, nursing espressos. Cady knew her dad would no doubt complain about the quality of the coffee later. For now, however, he appeared all ears.

Cassandra Told Me played a few songs and then Harry was introduced. By now, the room was almost filled to capacity. Cady's chest thumped when she realized she'd be singing in a matter of minutes.

Some singers would sit out in the crowd and mingle before a performance, but not Cady. She needed alone-time in order to prep for a performance. She stood off to the side, trying to keep a very low profile, although her eyes continued to scan the crowd for someone. She'd slipped one of her flyers into Lucas's locker that week. He said he'd come, but so far he was a no-show.

Harry played a brilliant set that featured some of his

own stuff as well as a few cover tunes, including a killer version of "Give Peace a Chance." Harry believed he was the reincarnation of John Lennon, which made most people laugh, especially when he wore his round spectacles and ratty black "New York City" T-shirt. Cady knew Harry was a bit of a poser, as were a lot of the singers and musicians here, but she thought it was all good fun. Dressing up was a part of the scene. Tonight Cady had even worn something special in honor of Lucas. She had tossed aside her typical T-shirt and jeans for a tight-fitting black tube top, choker, and long, loose pair of black pants with cowboy boots. Marisol had stepped in to tame Cady's hair, too, so it fell in a cascade of romantic curls instead of the usual tangle.

As soon as Harry finished, the crowd snapped their fingers together in the air like people used to do for beat poets in the 60s. The Big Cup owner claimed that snaps, not claps, were the best way to say "good job" at his place. But Cady called all that tiny applause. She preferred full-out clapping — the kind that brought people to their feet with a swell like a pounding heart.

"And now, we'd like to introduce one of Big Cup's regulars. Would you put your fingertips together for . . . Cady Sanchez."

Cady grabbed her guitar and strutted up to the stage. Snaps preceded her, along with a few loud whistles coming from Marisol and Bebe's table. She moved smoothly over to the bar stool at center stage and stepped into the single spotlight.

"Thanks," Cady said in a husky whisper. Although she

always got nerves before a gig, the moment she was onstage for real, the nervousness evaporated. All she could think about was singing.

The snaps died down, and Cady squinted at the spotlight. She could just barely make out the Big Cup tables, the light was that bright. She bobbed her head from side to side, still searching for Lucas. Maybe he was sitting way in the back? Against one wall, Cady did catch a glimpse of Dad's silhouette. She saw him giving her a big thumbs-up.

Cady strummed a few warm-up chords on the guitar and settled back onto the stool. She leaned forward just a little bit into the microphone.

"This is a new song, a song for . . ." Cady paused and the room seemed very quiet, breathless, as the audience waited for Cady's dedication.

She briefly thought about dedicating the song to "the guy who understands me, you know who you are" or something like that, because of course she couldn't pronounce Lucas Wheeler's name right out here in the open in front of everyone — including her father.

"Well, let me just get to it," Cady muttered, inhaling the sweet ginger smell of candles burning, rather than making any real dedication.

As Cady started to play, she hummed into the microphone. Her opening music sounded a little like a waterfall or trickling rain, a quick beat she'd stolen off a Wyndham Hill instrumental record in her dad's collection.

Then she began to sing in full voice.

Standing at the edge
Between there and here
My heart's a drum
You are the one

In the middle of the night
You take my hand, take my hand
In the middle of the flood
You are the land and everything in between
I'm stopped, I'm stung
I've come undone
And you move me
Closer to truth
We get each other
This much
And I say
This much
Is better than none

Standing at the edge
Between there and here
My heart's a drum
You are the one
You are the one

The snapping started as soon as she'd strummed her final chord. And there was clapping, too, just the way Cady liked it. She hopped off her stool for just a moment to readjust her black top and retune her guitar, and while she was standing outside the spotlight, once again Cady searched for Lucas.

She saw a bunch of faces that looked half-familiar. Then she saw Marisol and Bebe, grinning widely. She was on to the next song.

The remaining tunes seemed to go by quickly. When her set was over, the house lights went up, as dim as ever, and the kid in the beret thanked everyone for coming. Cady stood back, clutching her guitar tightly.

She could see everything now.

Lucas wasn't there, anywhere.

The room buzzed with the sound of voices and cups again. Cady's dad and her brother, Diego, pushed their way up to the stage, followed by Cady's friends. Harry was up front.

"That's your best set yet," Harry whispered to Cady. "Man, gotta love that first song. Did you write that about me?"

Cady had to laugh. "Yeah, Harry, how did you know?" she asked, flashing a wide smile and shaking off some of the discomfort she was having about Lucas not being there. Harry winked and disappeared off to the side to hang with the Cassandra Told Me sisters.

As soon as Cady hopped down off the stage, Dad grabbed her cheeks and then kissed each one.

"*¡Mi hija querida!*" Dad cried.

"Good job tonight, Cady," Diego mumbled. He wasn't one for emotional outbursts, not like Dad.

"Oh, *mi hija*! You get better every time I see you," Dad went on. "I am so proud. Too proud. *¡Felicitaciones!*"

"Yeah, you're a superstar, as usual," Diego groaned.

Dad flipped the back of Diego's ear. "Shut that mouth," he growled at his son. "Tonight is Cady's night."

Cady smiled sheepishly at Dad's gushing, and then rolled her eyes at Diego.

"You rocked the house," Marisol said, stepping up to Cady.

Bebe nodded. "Tony says you're the best one here," she said.

Tony shrugged. "Yeah, that's what I said."

Cady tugged on Marisol's shirt and pulled her close.

"Hey," she whispered in Marisol's ear. "By any chance did you see Lucas here earlier?"

Marisol cocked her head. "I don't think so, hon. But we were a little busy so maybe I just missed him. Or maybe he ducked in and left early . . ."

"Maybe," Cady said in a monotone voice.

But she knew the truth. The night had been about Cady's performance, not about Lucas showing up. Cady had to stop spending all this time worrying about a boy.

After all, someday Lucas would figure everything out. Someday he would understand the way Cady really felt — and the way she knew he had to feel, too. Someday Lucas would hear the slow song she'd written just for him.

And his heart would be a drum, too.

Chapter Thirteen

March 14, 1:18 PM
Hope

The air whipped around Hope's ankles, and she cursed the wind. She tasted her hair and bits of grit. Chesterfield Beach was empty today. Hardly anyone ever came here in the winter, and early March was technically still winter.

Today's beach was hard, cold, and unforgiving. Hope wished she'd brought another sweater. Up in the sky a fat seagull flapped its wings and screeched. Then a few more birds joined in, until the sky turned into a chorus of dives and swoops and squeals. All the activity left a light dusting of feathers on the packed-down sand. Hope half-expected one of the gulls to poop on her head — there were so many flying so close. She kept covering her head with her open palms, just in case.

Lucas was up ahead of Hope, chasing a few gulls off the beach. He kicked a plastic bottle that had washed up on the shore, and a cluster of birds scattered. Winter beaches always seemed full of garbage and residue and sludge from long-ago boat trips and melted snowdrifts. Most of it was junk or broken sea glass that got caught up in the jetty of rocks poking out from shore.

One time Hope had found a wallet on the beach, right here. It was intact — driver's license, Mobil gas card, everything. And even though she could have called the owner to return it, Hope had placed the wallet inside a plastic bag to keep as a souvenir. Hope wasn't much for journals or confessional poetry. Collecting things was the best way to catalog her own experiences. She kept a collection of decorative porcelain frogs in her bedroom like a lineup of potential prince charmings.

"Hurry up!" Lucas called to Hope over his shoulder. He was at least fifty yards away by now, and with the hard flap of wind, Hope could barely make out what he was saying.

Hope lifted her arm and waved for him to come back to her. She didn't want to go any farther down the beach than she had already walked. The goose pimples on her legs were beginning to feel more like pox or bug bites. She needed someplace that wasn't sandy so she could put her shoes back on again.

Lucas jogged back toward Hope. In his hand, he carried a medium-sized conch shell. He presented it to her with a grand flourish.

"From the sea, for thee," Lucas said, laughing at the rhyme.

Hope frowned. "But it's broken," she said. "Look. There's a crack and half of one side is missing."

"Not if you hold it this way," Lucas said, turning the shell back over again. "Look at the color. It's so pink — and pinker on the inside."

"It's broken," Hope repeated. "Why would I want that?"

Rolling his eyes, Lucas tossed the shell onto the hard sand. It rolled away soundlessly, and he looked after it, briefly, like he'd thrown away something important. Hope tugged on his shirttail to get him to keep walking.

They headed back to the main road at the lip of the waterfront, where the car was parked and where a restaurant and playground had recently been constructed. The new architecture—sleek benches, shiny swing set, and low green bushes—stood in stark contrast to the old, battered brown bathroom shed situated just a few feet away. It was one of those bathrooms where the cold cement floor is always wet and sandy, and the soap dispensers are out of soap, and a person can't *really* sit down on the toilet seat, so peeing turns into an Olympic gymnastics event.

From here, everything looked bare and exposed—a vast stretch of sand, rocks, and a thin line of foam as the tide surged. The only people who had ventured onto the beach were two joggers, a guy in a Mad Hatter hat carrying a clunky metal detector, and an old couple walking their dalmatian.

Hope made a beeline for one of the swings on the set. She brushed the damp sand off her feet and pulled on her shoes again. It felt good to warm up her toes. She sat back in the swing seat and pumped her legs until they lifted her up into the air.

"I want to swing," Hope called out to Lucas. "Come on."

She stared at the back of Lucas's head. His thoughts seemed lost in the horizon. Lucas wasn't the same these past few weeks, and Hope knew why: Cady Sanchez.

Lately, despite Hope's protests, Lucas had been spending a lot of his free time with Cady, dreaming up songs.

"Lucas, I said come and *swing* with me!" Hope yelled to him again.

This time, Lucas heard her and came over to his own swing. He leaned back in the rubber sling and pushed off the gravel below. Soon, he and Hope were swinging in perfect synchronicity.

"Where are you?" Hope asked, sailing into midair, legs dangling. She remembered back to her days as a kid when she'd try to go higher and higher on the swing in her own backyard. There was no better feeling than flying through the air — so close to letting everything go.

Lucas didn't answer. He was still gazing out at the water.

Hope didn't like being ignored. She dropped her feet to the ground, kicking up stones. "Let's go," she announced abruptly.

"Go?" Lucas stopped.

"I'm bored," Hope said.

"How can you be bored with all this?" He gestured out toward the ocean, where the tide roughed up the shoreline. Debris blew around in circles like tornadoes on the sand.

"Lucas, I want to go," Hope complained. "The sky is getting dark. Isn't it supposed to rain? I've had enough."

"Maybe you just need someone to warm you up," Lucas said, grinning.

"You wish," Hope said.

"No. *You* wish," Lucas replied, coming over to where she still sat on her swing.

Hope smiled. She liked it when Lucas acted cocky. "You said that you had a surprise for me today. What is it?" she asked suggestively.

"A surprise does not always mean a thing," Lucas said, kneeling down in front of her. He reached for her neck, but his fingertips were ice.

"Stop. That's cold," Hope said, shrugging his hand away.

"Let's go back to your car," Lucas said. He placed his hands on top of her thighs.

"I've been thinking," Hope said. "Maybe we should tell people about us."

"Us?" Lucas cried. "You don't mean that."

"How do you know what I mean?" Hope asked, placing her hands on top of his.

"Come here," Lucas said. He pulled forward gently to kiss her.

"You want me, don't you?" Hope teased.

Lucas had a dumb grin on his face. "What else would I want?"

"If you really want me, then catch me!" Hope said, standing up and breaking away. Lucas fell backward onto his butt.

Laughing, Hope danced away from the swings, past the curving green plastic-covered slides, and beyond. She found a long metal bench with a perfect view of the sea. Her feet tapped their own rhythm; she pulled her hands up into her sleeves and waited.

Lucas chased Hope so fast that he collapsed face-first onto the bench. He flipped over and squinted. The sun was in his eyes.

Hope sucked in the ocean air. "I'm surprised you haven't said anything about Cady today," she said.

"Cady?" Lucas said. "Why should I say anything about her?"

"You tell me."

"No. Why don't you tell me? Aren't you guys in the same play?"

Hope nodded. "So."

"So? What's this about?"

"I know you've been seeing Cady Sanchez, too, Lucas. You don't have to keep up your lie."

"Of course I see her. We're friends. She's a musician like me. That's it."

"Right," Hope said coldly.

Lucas pulled back a little when she said that. He made a face. "You know how much music matters to me, Hope," he said.

"You talk about your music," Hope said. "But that's all just code words for Cady."

"What the hell is your problem?" Lucas said, sounding annoyed.

"Don't play with me, Lucas."

"Play with you?" Lucas asked. "I told you before. Cady's cool but there's no spark. It's not like that. It's not like us."

"Us?" Hope asked.

"Hope, I'm in love with *you.*"

Hope bristled. She wanted to seize Lucas by the throat and shout "YOU'RE A BIG FAT STUPID LIAR!" After all, she'd seen it — them — with her own eyes. From outside Blue Notes yesterday, Hope had seen Lucas and Cady walking into one of the listening booths, their bodies pressed together. And she could not get that picture out of her mind. After everything she'd said and done, Hope could not believe it had come to this. She needed to make Lucas pay.

A gull flapped by, and Hope leaped off the bench and threw her arms into the air, too, like a bird, daring Lucas to follow her back to the hard sand, back to the beach. The wind had died down some by now, so she got a good running start.

Lucas gave chase. He was more like a retriever today, pounding along behind Hope, mouth half open. "Where are you going?" he yelled. "I thought you were cold. I thought you wanted to go."

Hope's feet thumped on the sand as she ran awkwardly toward the water's edge. Her blond hair flew about her face, still sticking to her mouth and nose. She was out of breath before she'd run too far. Smoking cigarettes made her slower at running, but that wasn't a good enough reason for her to quit.

Lucas had just about caught up. At the last moment he accelerated so quickly toward Hope that he pushed her down before he even had a chance to stop short.

Hope flew. When she came to a crash landing, she had damp sand everywhere: in her ears, in her hair, down her shirt. She spit some out of her mouth as Lucas climbed onto her.

"What are you doing?" Hope asked, trying to shift away.

But Lucas was heavy. He pressed her wrists onto the beach, fingers rounded like handcuffs. "You can't get away from me," he said.

He leaned into Hope's face but then pulled back with alarm. "Crap!" he cried, reaching for his earlobe. "What did you do that for?"

Hope had bit him. Hard. They stared at each other, pie-eyed.

"You're crazy," Lucas said, still clearly shaken from the nip.

"Maybe." Hope smiled. "But isn't that why you love me — if you really *do* love me?"

"I do," Lucas said, fingering his ear again. "I just —"

Hope grabbed his shoulders and kissed his mouth. Touching him made her forget about the sand and the cold — just for a moment. He pressed his entire body back down onto hers. Hope felt something next to her head. Lucas reached for it, a sharp piece of shell sticking out of the sand.

Then he leaned back into Hope's mouth, harder than before. She let him lie there, kissing her, for almost a minute. Then he stopped.

"What is it?" Lucas asked, sitting up, wiping his chin. "You're not kissing back."

Hope looked into his eyes, but she didn't speak.

"What is going on?" Lucas asked.

"You know."

"I don't know. You're acting so different."

A piece of dried-out seaweed swept past them. The gulls came closer now. Hope's eyes scanned the wide sky.

"Let me up," Hope demanded.

"Why?"

"Let me up, I said. *Now.*"

Hope stood up and brushed off the sand and whatever else had attached itself to her body while she'd been lying there. If she'd had a referee whistle, she would have blown it. She shook out her hair and flipped it backward. She needed a shampoo.

Time was up.

Hope turned and started the short trek back across the beach to the parking lot. She knew Lucas was right behind her, arms whisking through the air. For a runner, he had sloppy form. Hope was always telling him to keep his chin up, keep his back straight, and keep his arms loose. But he didn't listen. He insisted on doing things his way.

Now it was time to do things *her* way.

"Hope! Stop," Lucas called out, but Hope ignored him. She tried to get her feet to move a little bit faster, but the wind had picked up again. Luckily the cars weren't too far away now. She could see Lucas's convertible on one side, her Volkswagen on the other. They always took two cars anytime they met. It made the getting to and getting back easier. It also reduced the chances of their being seen together. She held up her hands so she wouldn't get blowing-around sand in her eyes.

"HOPE!" Lucas screamed as soon as Hope stepped off the sandy beach onto the blacktop.

He screamed her name a few times, probably because he couldn't hear as well with all the wind and sand.

"HOPE, HOLD UP!"

Hope got to his car first. She perched on his bumper, wrapping her shirt around her middle.

"What . . . the . . . what's . . . going on?" Lucas asked, breathless, when he walked up to the car.

"I think this is good-bye, Lucas," Hope replied.

"Good-bye? What?" Lucas started to laugh. Then he unlocked the car door. "Let's get inside," he said. "It's warm inside."

Hope shivered. "I'm not going anywhere with you."

Lucas leaned down and grabbed her wrist. He pulled her up toward him. "Come on," he insisted.

He jammed into the backseat and pulled her close. The leather seats were clammy with the damp cold.

"Is this some kind of trick?" Lucas said, half-laughing nervously. "I can't figure you out."

"Not many people can," Hope said with a boastful tone. But she wasn't laughing. "You realize, Lucas, that out of everyone in Chesterfield, I'm your only real friend," Hope continued. "I bet I'm the only person here who knows the real you."

"I have other friends," Lucas said, still chuckling.

"Not like me. There will never be anyone like me."

Lucas sat back. "Oh yeah?"

He leaned in to unfasten the buttons on her polo T-shirt and the clasp on the front of her lace bra.

"Turn on the car. Turn on the heat," Hope ordered.

Lucas didn't have to be asked twice. He leaned into the front seat as requested. The car pumped hot air into the back.

"I have to go to work after this, you know," Hope said.

"This won't take long," Lucas said, grinning.

Hope moved the seat belt strap and lay back on the car seat. She knew he was all worked up — and inside, so was she. Lucas was the only boy Hope had ever known who really knew what to do with his hands — and tongue. With a single tug, she pulled her T-shirt up to her ears and over her head and opened her bra with a loud snap.

Lucas gasped like he always did when he touched Hope's bare chest. Then he took off his own shirt.

Hope looked close. She examined the pattern of scars on Lucas's flat stomach. He had told her so many times where some of them came from, but she never believed anything Lucas said about them or anything else. She believed the scars were nothing more than cuts Lucas made himself to look tough — tougher than he really was.

Cady had stared at those same scars, hadn't she?

Hope imagined how Cady's lips must have kissed them, kissed him. She imagined Cady and Lucas playing guitar together at school, singing in perfect harmony, sitting on the couch at that party way back on New Year's, and then pressed together at Blue Notes.

Hope had seen it all.

Lucas had his eyes closed as he started to kiss her collarbone down to her stomach, but Hope kept her eyes open — wide open — so she could keep on seeing everything. She kept her eyes open until Lucas stopped. She kept her eyes open so she could see right through the fogged windows of the car, watching the sky get very dark, even though it was still the middle of the day.

There was never turning back once something started. And she'd been the one to start *all* of this, back at the

New Year's Eve party, so it was her job to stop, too, whenever she wanted. Hope's actions were like a storm darkening, bearing down on Lucas and everyone else. She was in charge of everyone and everything—including the rain.

Chapter Twelve

March 6, 11:34 AM
Lucas

The outside of Blue Notes music store was like a movie set piece, complete with neon signs, shiny brass instruments hanging from pegs in the window, and wallpaper with a notes and keys design. This place was the perfect combination of nostalgia meets technology; it proudly displayed Victrolas alongside iPods. There were even custom-designed listening booths where customers could sample hot new songs in soundproof little closets. Only recently, the store had also added a small coffee bar, which made it like a Barnes & Noble for sound.

Adjacent to Blue Notes was the Crestwood Music Center, a training school where mostly amateurs and grade-schoolers learned to strum a guitar or play piano for the very first time. Cady worked there as a teacher for extra cash and a megadiscount on music supplies. Lucas always teased Cady about the fact that she spent so much time at the Center that she called the manager Uncle Vince, as if he were a real member of her family.

Getting to know a girl like Cady Sanchez in the middle of the school year had overwhelmed Lucas at first. While most other people he knew dreamed in pictures, Cady dreamed in scales and chords, just like he did.

For as long as he could remember, Lucas had been

acutely tuned in to the sound track of his own life. When he was only five, he got a Fisher-Price microphone and tape recorder and began experimenting with sounds. First he'd record birds, trucks, and water trickling from the sink faucet. Then he'd make up his own stories to go with the sounds. In grammar school, instead of playing video games, Lucas would hunt for noises. He'd read somewhere that even the highest-tech sounds were grounded in the ordinary: a vacuum cleaner on the floor, glass breaking, or the low gurgle of a hungry baby. Lucas once read that one of the top sound engineers for the *Star Wars* movies traveled and taped sounds all over the world just to get the right sound for each film. That guy called himself a sound collector, and that was the kind of life Lucas could imagine for himself.

It wasn't just sounds of daily life that Lucas loved. It was music, too, of course. These days hip-hop was close to the top of his list, but he would blast Bach in the car, too. He wore only black for his entire sophomore year as a tribute to Johnny Cash.

That was the same year his mother died.

Lucas knew he'd gotten his love of music from his mother, Abby. She never turned off the radio, no matter where she was. It was on inside the car. It was on inside the kitchen. She even purchased one of those waterproof radios for the shower. Lucas's dad always said that Abby's mezzo-soprano voice rivaled the most beautiful songbirds. She wasn't really a performer, but to Lucas, at age five and then seven and then ten, and right before the accident, she was *his* songbird. She had bought Lucas his first drum set, taken him to his first concert (*Sesame Street*), and purchased his first piece of sheet music (John Lennon's "Yesterday"). Although Abby died, Lucas still remained determined to keep the music — *her* music — alive.

One Saturday in the driving rain, Lucas met Cady at Blue Notes, just by chance. They had each come for different reasons, but they ended up huddled together in the back of the shop with oversized cardboard cups of coffee, talking and poring over volumes of old sheet music that the store had on display.

"You know the assistant principal approached me to write a song for prom," Cady said. "And at first I was really flattered, but then I wasn't totally sure how to feel or what to think. I mean, why would he ask me to write a song, you know?"

Sometimes Cady spoke without taking a breath, words falling one into the other like tipped dominoes, and there was very little Lucas could do to stop any of it.

"And then I thought to myself: How am I supposed to write a song for prom? Doesn't the whole notion of prom music seem to go against everything we stand for musically? I mean, I know it's a good opportunity to get my stuff out there — any event is — but do I really want to play songs for a bunch of kids dressed up in chiffon and ties? Do I really care what half the student population thinks about my music?"

"Uh . . ." Lucas said thoughtfully. "Actually, I think you do."

"Yeah, I guess I do."

They laughed together, and without really thinking,

Lucas slipped his fingers into the thick brown hair that drooped over Cady's forehead.

Cady sat up straighter, surprised by the touch.

"Uh . . . I just wanted to see your face," Lucas explained, withdrawing his hand.

"Oh," Cady said. She tucked the loose hair behind her ear. "I'm such a mess today. My hair loves the rain, can't you tell? Say hello to the giant frizz-ball."

"You are not a mess," Lucas said as nicely as he could.

Cady smiled. "Thanks."

A small group of children came into Blue Notes after one of their morning classes at the Center. Cady knew at least half of the kids, and so she waved to them, blowing kisses. Lucas knew that if he ever had to teach a class to a bunch of eight-year-olds, he'd need to down a Valium or some beers first. But Cady was naturally good with kids. She didn't need any help.

"So have you written this loathed prom song yet?" Lucas asked.

"I've started four. I can't finish any of them. I actually got stuck on the best word to rhyme with limousine."

"Seventeen? Mean? Obscene?" Lucas said.

"Ha ha," Cady said.

"Pick one song out of a hat," Lucas joked. "Does it really matter? Just play a cover of a Carpenters' tune, or maybe Yanni."

"Very funny," Cady said. "That would be one way to get everyone to hate me at the same time."

"They already do," Lucas teased, poking Cady in the shoulder.

"Great," Cady said. She tried to be upbeat, but Lucas could hear in Cady's voice that she didn't feel like making fun.

"Why don't you just play the song of yours that won that award?" Lucas asked, trying to offer some real advice.

Cady's eyes lit up and a smile spread across her face. "Oh my God. Lucas, you're totally right. Why didn't I think of that? Then I don't need to make up something new."

"Yeah, you're big into recycling anyway, aren't you?" Lucas joked again.

A loud boom shook the building.

"Thunder," Cady said. She craned her neck to see out the window of the store. "It's so dark outside it's practically like night. I'm glad we're in here out of the rain."

"Me too," Lucas said.

He meant it two ways. Lucas was glad to be in out of the cold rain, but he was also glad, genuinely glad, to be sharing this afternoon with Cady. Lately he'd been spending so much free time with Hope, he'd almost forgotten how good a friend Cady could be.

"Lucas, can I ask you something?"

Lucas nodded.

"Do you think I should go to prom?"

"Of course you should go."

Cady grinned. "I just get a little insecure this time of year. I really hate these things. But I want to go."

"I want to go, too."

Cady slouched backward on the couch where she and

Lucas sat. Her flared pants had wet cuffs from puddles. Lucas's own Levis were still damp, too.

Nearby, speakers played the second movement from Wagner's "Ride of the Valkyries."

"I love this piece. You know that scene where the helicopters fly out of the sky and ride over the water in *Apocalypse Now*?" Lucas asked.

"I've never seen it," Cady said.

"Are you kidding me?"

"Mom said it was a little heavy."

"Heavy? You're so funny," Lucas said.

"Why am I funny?"

"You haven't seen that flick. You told me last week that you've never ridden a horse."

"I don't like horses."

"There are all these things you haven't done."

"Like what?"

"I don't know. Bungee jumping. Platform diving."

"And you've done these things?" Cady asked.

Lucas shrugged. "Actually, yeah. But I know most kids haven't. I just did them because I traveled with my dad. You know, after my mom died. He took me away a lot."

Cady chewed on a nail. Lucas knew she was uncomfortable, but he kept at it.

"Look, I know you like to play this little girl thing . . ."

"Little girl?"

"Wide-eyed, innocent, that whole scene."

"Me?" Cady looked shocked. "It's not like I'm dressing in virginal white every day."

"Buuuuut . . ." Lucas said, raising an eyebrow.

Cady leaned closer to him. "But what?"

"I think you should get a tattoo."

Cady exploded into laughter. "What does a tattoo have to do with anything?"

"Everything," Lucas said, grinning.

Cady sat back and rolled her eyes. "Sometimes, Lucas, you have this bad boy thing, but . . ."

She stopped mid-sentence.

"But what?" Lucas said, chuckling.

"Well, I think *you* should get a tattoo, too."

Lucas stroked the stubble on his chin. "I already have one."

Cady's eyes opened wide. "Where?"

Lucas twisted to the side and lifted up the hem of the faded green polo shirt that he wore over a long-sleeved gray tee. When he raised the polo, Cady saw his washboard abs and the waistband of his jersey boxers.

"Say hello to Mr. Tattoo," Lucas said, tugging down the elastic waist in front. A little farther to the right and he'd be revealing a lot more than just skin.

Cady giggled even more when she saw his tattoo up close. She examined the small black ink image of a yin-yang symbol near his pelvis.

"You like?" he asked. "I got it last year on a dare. My friend Danny and I got wasted one night and . . . uh, long story."

Cady couldn't speak, she was giggling so much.

"What's so funny?" Lucas asked.

"Nothing's funny, not really," Cady explained. "I just didn't expect to see . . . well . . ."

"Say no more," Lucas said teasingly. "No compliments on my pecs or my quads or other incredible body parts. Really, I'm not looking for . . ."

Cady's giggling was off the charts by now.

"Stop. Stop. They're going to throw us out," Lucas said.

"Is someone looking over here?" Cady asked, hiccupping.

"Cady, I was kidding," Lucas said. People moved around the store, but no one was looking directly at them. The only other person Lucas could see was a tall Indian man with a turban standing at the customer service counter.

"Whew. How embarrassing," Cady said. "I thought I was going to wet my pants."

"Thanks for sharing," Lucas said.

Cady leaned back into the pillows behind her on the store sofa, and Lucas moved forward, ever so slightly, until his face was as close as it could be next to hers without touching. He could see from the look in Cady's eyes that she hadn't expected him to do that. He turned his head and rested it on the pillow next to hers.

Now we're breathing the same air, Lucas thought.

He liked it.

Up real close, this close, Cady smelled like sandalwood or patchouli. He couldn't decide which. Her skin was smoother, too, than it looked from a distance, and she wasn't even wearing makeup. Hope White always wore lipstick and mascara and blush, but Cady didn't cover up.

Until today, Lucas had never noticed so many of the little details of her face. One of Cady's eyes was bigger than the other.

"Hey," Lucas whispered.

"Hey," Cady said, aping him.

"Have you . . . heard the new John Legend?" Lucas asked. When Cady shook her head, Lucas suggested that they slip into one of the back booths to listen to the disc. Cady stood up with him and grabbed two sets of headphones as they moved into an empty booth.

Lucas pushed a few buttons on a console and punched in a secret listener code. The display lit up with green and orange. Then the music poured into the booth with its hard bass line and melody like sweet cream.

Lucas moved in time to the music. He stared at Cady.

"I never noticed how you have these little flecks of yellow in your eyes," Cady said, watching him closely. "It's nice."

Her hips were moving from side to side.

"I was thinking the same thing about you," Lucas replied. "Your eyes are beautiful."

"What a line," Cady said.

"You said it first," Lucas said.

"I know."

"But I meant it."

Lucas leaned in and he pressed his lips onto Cady's. He started with one deep, long kiss and then smaller ones, all around her mouth. Something about her lips tasted sweet, like berries. Her neck smelled like the rain.

As he leaned back again, Lucas traced a fingertip across

Cady's soft mouth, down her chin and neck. He gently hooked the finger under the top of Cady's sweater, revealing a shoulder.

"What's this?" Lucas asked. He saw a cluster of freckles there, begging to be touched. Lucas slid his hands down beyond the shoulder, down her arm, past her waist.

"Oh." Cady looked up into his eyes and pushed away his hand. "We should stop."

Lucas stared, mouth hanging open. He'd been so ready for this first kiss — and more — but Cady's arm crossed in front like a road sign.

Yield. Do Not Enter. STOP.

Lucas had taken only one step and already he'd gone too far?

"I'm sorry," Cady said, more embarrassed than she'd been before the kiss. "I just didn't expect —"

"N-no . . ." Lucas stammered. "My bad. That was weird, right?"

Cady didn't say anything and Lucas tried to laugh it off. He reached out and lightly patted her arm.

"You okay?" Lucas asked gently.

"I should go get my guitar," Cady blurted. "I forgot it. In the car."

"Sure," Lucas responded. "Your guitar."

Over their heads, outside Blue Notes, another thunderbolt rumbled, like some kind of punctuation. Lucas wondered if it was an exclamation point or a question mark.

Chapter Eleven

March 4, 3:02 PM
Cady

"So, has he done anything yet?" Marisol asked Cady.

They sat together at a table near a window in the school cafeteria, pretending to work on a calculus worksheet, noshing on a bag of Cheetos, and dissecting the events of the previous week. Chesterfield had a row of Snapple vending machines at the back of the room, so kids could get a sugar buzz during free periods or after classes.

Cady twirled a strand of hair around her fingers and took a sip of Wango Mango.

"Define what you mean by 'done anything,'" she replied.

Marisol balked. "Cady! You're kidding, right? Lucas Wheeler has been in your orbit since New Year's. He calls you. He e-mails you. He IMs you. So why hasn't he kissed you yet? Why doesn't he *do* anything?"

Cady shrugged. "We came close."

"Close doesn't cut it," Marisol said, making a chopping motion at her neck. "This dude better act fast or you need to say *adios* and look elsewhere, my friend."

"Look elsewhere for what?"

"What do you think?"

"It's not all about sex," Cady said.

Marisol made a *tsk-tsk-tsk* sound. "You wish it weren't."

"Excuse me, Queen of the Cynics," Cady groaned, rolling her eyes.

"I'm not cynical, I'm realistic," Marisol said. "Unlike your other friend Hope."

"Why do you always trash her?" Cady asked.

"Because she is so trashable. Don't you see it?"

Cady shook her head. "I think she's nice, actually. I mean, she's nice to me."

"Only because she wants something from you."

"Like I said, Queen of the Cynics."

Marisol's head dropped down and she got very quiet.

"What's wrong now?" Cady asked.

"I just remembered that I forgot to call Ed."

"The guy from your lit class?"

Marisol nodded. "Yeah."

Cady's eyes got wide. "But, Mari, last time I checked you'd decided that he was sort of attractive but in a friendly way. You said it was no frills. What did I miss?"

Marisol sighed. "I've been trying hard not to like him. I really have. I mean, the last thing I wanted for senior year was some kind of serious relationship. But Ed smells so good, Cady. He smells like limes or something so yummy. And he's such a long way from Rodrigo. Remember? Rigo always smelled like his part-time gig at McDonald's."

Cady laughed out loud. Then she thought about the way Lucas smelled.

"I think Ed could be it, Cady."

"*It?* You've been dating him for five minutes."

"I've known him since third grade."

Cady rolled her eyes.

"This is no fling."

"Okay, tell me everything," Cady insisted.

Marisol never talked about romance like this. She prided herself on being the party girl. But in talking about her new relationship with Ed, Marisol's eyes softened. Her voice softened.

"First of all, he got me flowers," Marisol explained. "Why didn't someone tell me how *good* it would feel if someone gave me a handful of daisies? It felt *so* good."

"What were the flowers for?" Cady asked.

"He didn't say. That's the best part."

"That is so Cary Grant. Or so Hugh Grant," Cady said.

Marisol laughed. "But it's weird, right? I like bad boys. Edgy. You're the one who likes the bleeding hearts."

"I do not," Cady said. "Lucas isn't a bleeding heart."

"Oh, please. He walks around with that 'My dad was some Navy tough guy' thing going on. Inside, he's grape jelly, just like you."

Cady took another sip of her drink. "So have you and Ed . . . you know . . . been together?"

"Of course," Marisol said. "I don't like guys unless I try them on for size. You know me."

Cady laughed. Marisol talked about sex like it was kissing. Everything was one big casual hook-up, to be continued.

"Where?" Cady asked.

"His car. And then on the back porch of my grand-mother's house."

"Oh my God! Marisol!"

Marisol held her hands up in front of her face. "I know. He was dropping me off and I couldn't exactly bring him upstairs to meet Nana, so we found the next best place."

Cady gasped again. She could never do that. She'd barely even touched a guy down there, and even then it was only in a closet during a wild summer party when she'd made the horrendous mistake of doing three shots of tequila and finishing two beers. The only thing Cady remembered was watching the wall vibrate and feeling dizzy and lying down in the middle of a room until she was utterly freaked out by the fact that some guy she didn't even know had his tongue in her ear and she had her hand down his pants and less than no idea about how it got there. Cady hated the idea that she'd lost so much control in the span of one night, and she vowed never to lose control again.

Never.

Marisol glanced up at the clock on the wall of the cafeteria and let out a loud groan. "Oh, Cade, I'm sorry to leave you like this, but I totally forgot I have to babysit today," Marisol said. "Call me later. We can finish the problem set over the phone. Okay?"

"Okay," Cady said. She stood up from the table. Her body felt heavy, as if she had tin cans in her pockets and rocks tied to her sneakers. The last place in the world she felt like going was to practice for her role in the school production of *The Children's Hour*. But she headed up the staircase toward the drama room. Although the final show would be performed in the school auditorium, their rehearsals took place in a smaller classroom. The only problem with that arrangement was the fact that some rehearsing involved props, which were inconveniently located backstage.

Today, Cady needed to get a phone prop. She walked into the auditorium. The aisles were narrow and so dimly lit that Cady wasn't one-hundred percent sure where she was walking.

"Hello?" Cady called out to anyone who would hear. But no one responded.

The backstage area was cramped, but efficient. Heavy, crimson curtains hung across the diameter of the stage. Behind those were other stage doors and prop windows. And behind that were two other real doors: one to the cast dressing room and one to the prop room.

Both doors were always left unlocked.

Except today.

When Cady tried to open the prop closet, the door stuck. She twisted the knob and leaned with her elbow in a futile attempt to push the door open.

"Great," Cady muttered under her breath.

All at once, the door opened.

Cady stepped back as Rich Walsh, one of the stage managers, stepped out.

"Sorry," Rich mumbled. He was pulling up his pants zipper. He kept right on moving.

Cady pushed the door open all the way.

"Hello?" she called out as she went inside. "Is someone else in here?"

"Hey."

Across the small room, Hope sat in a gilded, velvet-covered chair. She had one foot up on a carton filled with hats and was lacing up a tall brown leather boot.

Cady was tongue-tied. She'd expected to find someone else in the closet, but she hadn't expected it to be Hope.

"What are you doing here?" Cady asked.

"Well, I'm not doing my homework."

Cady didn't say a word.

"I'm kidding, Cady. I was just getting ready for rehearsal."

"With Rich?"

"What does it look like?"

"Aren't you afraid you'll get caught?" Cady asked.

"Um . . . no."

By now, Hope had laced up her other boot. She stood up from the chair, picked up a pile of four or five books, and started to make her way out of the room. Cady noticed how Hope swung her hips when she moved.

"What if a teacher had walked in instead of me?" Cady asked.

"Like that's going to happen."

"So are you and Rich going out?"

"Oh my God, Cady, what are you—a quiz show? Don't be so naïve. I was just having a good time. Can't you just relax?"

Hope pushed past Cady and disappeared into the backstage area.

"Oh, well . . . see you at rehearsal," Cady said, flustered.

After she'd gone, Cady sat down in the red upholstered chair that Hope had been sitting in. Memories of seventh grade flooded back, including the hundred-and-one reasons why Cady and Hope had ceased to be friends.

Cady sat there for a moment and then headed to the rehearsal.

When she walked into the room, Hope was leaning on the window ledge between two potted plants, with her cell phone flipped open to talk. Cell phones weren't allowed in classes, but they were fair game at play rehearsal. At least six kids were talking on them right now.

As Hope animatedly spoke into her cell, she threw her head back and laughed. Today she wore a pink baby doll camisole with a pair of shredded, bleach-stained jeans that hugged her in all the right places. Cady sighed. If only she could bottle Hope's glow and reapply it to herself like quick-tanning lotion.

Cady pulled out a teeny notebook that she'd stashed in her pocket. A song was on the wing, although Cady wasn't exactly sure where it was flying from. She crossed her legs, sat on the floor, closed her eyes, and pictured Lucas. Then Cady took out her favorite black pen.

Do you know the truth about the sky?
It goes on and on and on
And so should we

Cady looked up from her notebook and stared at the other people in the room. She had always believed that writing songs would bring her closer to understanding people around her. But sometimes it did the opposite. The words built upon one another like bricks and mortar.

Cady looked over toward Hope, who had clicked her phone shut by now. She expected Hope to turn the other way, jump off her windowsill, and melt into the rest of the crowd. But instead, Hope caught Cady's eye. She smiled and walked over.

"Sorry about before, about upstairs," Hope said.

Cady nodded. "Me too. I didn't mean to interrupt."

"It's not like Rich cares," Hope whispered. "To be honest, no one cares, Cady. Everyone does it."

"Yeah," Cady said.

"Yeah."

"Who was on the phone just now?"

"Just some guy. But like I told you, no one cares. It's all casual."

"Oh," Cady said. For some reason, she cared.

"You look sort of silly sitting over here with your nose in a notebook," Hope said. "Why don't you stand with everyone else? I mean, we are in this play together, aren't we?"

Cady smiled. "Of course," she said, still not moving.

"Are you looking for a formal invitation?" Hope extended her hand. "Let's go."

And with one simple gesture and a few simple words from Hope, the brick wall that Cady kept raising was razed, just like that, and all the songs broke open, right along with Cady's heart.

Now everything was up for grabs.

Chapter Ten

March 2, 4:17 PM
Lucas

Hands slapping his thighs, Lucas pounded the pavement. His soccer coach had warned him about getting into a cardio slump during the winter, so here he was, determined to get his mileage up before spring officially arrived.

His breath was pure steam as he ran along. He circled one of the rotaries in the area, trying to steady his footfalls. His form was crap today and he knew it.

Three more miles.

Lucas took the big hill in the center of town, panting as he passed by the hardware store, the post office, Little Sisters of Great Charity consignment shop, Marty's Floral, a new deli, and a hole-in-the-wall Mexican restaurant called Amigos. Lucas's stomach grumbled at the thought of a fresh burrito, refried beans, and rice. On top of everything else, he was hungry.

Two miles and three-quarters.

What was his heart rate? Lucas could feel his chest *pum-pum* pounding, but he'd forgotten to bring the special watch with the heart monitor on it. Dad had purchased it for him after Lucas won his first 5K.

Dad was full of incentives like that. But it didn't mean anything to Lucas. After all, Dad would mix his gifts with loud, stern, "my way or the highway" commands, which made it awfully hard to see the good. Dad had been with the Navy for nearly twenty years before being honorably discharged, and he seemed to blame everyone in the world for his leaving — except himself. Luckily, Mr. Wheeler had enough family money to afford life's luxuries. But Lucas knew his dad's heart was crushed, so what was the point? First he lost his life's work. Then he lost his life's love.

The road curved into a cemetery, and Lucas jogged past the headstones, running to the rhythm of his own breath. He felt like the big bad wolf, huffing and puffing his way over small paths of slush and dirty ice left over from the big snow a few days before. He read the stones: Mortimer, Scagnelli, Jerold, Hirsch, Kramer. There was the chiseled cross standing at the fresh grave of a small boy who'd died just last week after getting hit by a bus. Lucas had seen a picture of the boy's sweet, young face in the paper.

Death really didn't discriminate, did it?

He thought about his mother's grave, back in Massachusetts, set up high on a hill next to her own parents. Lucas had never known those grandparents.

Two miles.

Since his mother died, Lucas had watched Dad mourn with a fervent obsession. He was angry almost all the time; yet he would not date again, even when Lucas begged him to do so. Aunt Rita had begged, too. She'd fixed up Dad with a woman from her real estate office. But Dad decided it was better to hang with the boys down at Reilly's instead of, as he put it, meeting some new babe.

So it went, year after dateless year.

That had been part of the reason for all the therapy back in Massachusetts, hadn't it? And the move: the attempt to begin again, closer to where Aunt Rita lived. She'd made arrangements for a new doctor, but lately Lucas had been skipping sessions. He had other things to fill his time, better things, flesh-and-blood things, not just crap talk about feelings and anxiety and fitting in.

The road forked and Lucas ran to the left, around a hydrant, and onto a sidewalk that had broken into pieces. He ran on, past a row of old Victorian homes painted in teals and deep purples and dark reds, with wide front porches and widow's walks. Up in the top floor of one house, Lucas saw a face pressed up against the window. A white-haired woman stared down at the street. He wondered if she was there alone. She looked so alone.

The streets of this new town didn't feel all that different from the streets Lucas had left behind in his neighborhood in Massachusetts. They curved into one another, like arms embracing him as he ran along. The style of the houses changed as Lucas turned onto Walker Street, his gait steady, arms fluid. He was finding his rhythm at last, even with all the ice. He picked up the pace a little, to nine-and-a-half-minute miles instead of ten. His best miles usually hovered around eight minutes. How could he ever run sub-seven-minute miles for all twenty-six marathon miles? That was the only way he would see the Boston Marathon.

One mile.

Now that his body was warmed up, moving along

smoothly, Lucas wondered why he hadn't joined the cross-country team at Chesterfield. Why had he gone for soccer instead? He'd made so many snap decisions since arriving in Chesterfield. School classes, sports, girls. Everything was surging forward this year. Did he really have control over any of it?

He remembered what his friend Frank had said before Lucas had left Baker, his old school. Frank said that Lucas was chipping off a piece of himself that he'd never get back again. Frank was into metaphors like that. As editor of the school paper, Frank had an exacting eye for all the painful details. All the "shit stuff" was what Lucas called it.

And Frank had been right, of course. Since he'd moved to Chesterfield with Dad at the end of last summer, Lucas had hardly spoken to any old pals from the cross-country team back at Baker. He'd walked away from cousins and uncles and neighbors he'd known since he was a kid. He'd walked away from friends like Frank and Chester and Enrique and Molly. He'd walked away from Rebecca, his girlfriend of four years.

No, no. He'd *run* away.

Half a mile.

As he turned another corner, climbing up a hill, the winter wind hit Lucas in the gut. He smelled burning. Someone (everyone?) had lit a fireplace, and the air teemed with the scent of cedar and pinecones. Lucas paced himself as he moved through another neighborhood, where rows of Tudor homes tucked in snugly together with their pitched roofs, leaded glass, and brick faces. Lucas searched the skies for the chimneys that were smoking.

Pum-pum. Pum-pum.

His heart was steady; his breath was full. This was a good workout. His head was clear. His mind was free. Good.

Lucas heard music inside his head. It was one of the songs from the mix CD that Cady had made for him. She'd packed it with "chick music" as a joke, but much to Lucas's surprise, he was beginning to like the Ani DiFranco and Sleater-Kinney cuts. Liking Cady's music was one of the Chesterfield changes that surprised Lucas the most. After all, next to running, music was the most sacred institution in Lucas's life; and he didn't let just anyone in.

And deep down, he knew Cady Sanchez wasn't just anyone, but still.

Lucas felt his side cramp—just a little bit—and he reached for it, twisting to make the pinch go away. *Breathe deep*, he told himself, continuing on with the run. He looked way up into the clouds over his head.

Lucas had decided long ago that the last person on earth who he wanted to be was his father. But here he was. There were the signs: all this running; the same ribald, throaty laugh; the same size-twelve feet; the same desire to love hard.

Where was he going now?

His sneakers began to skid, and in an instant Lucas was flat-footed, eyes searching the street signs to figure out his precise location. He started to choke on the cold air just a little bit, too, as he slowed down. This whole area looked familiar. Of course. He *had* meant to come here, hadn't he?

Lucas came to an abrupt stop, hands on his hips. He

bent over. It was cold out but his legs were slick with sweat underneath his ebony Nike running pants. He needed a shower. The stitch in his side was back. He exhaled deeply.

The mailbox on the post in front of Lucas was painted on the side with a bird's nest like in one of those *Hearth and Home* catalogs, and had curlicue designed numbers and letters. It said: 232 MEADOW LN, and on top of that, one short name: WHITE.

Lucas had already run past this house three times today, ten times yesterday. He gazed up at the shingles painted a dingy gray. The whole house looked asleep. Then, all at once, a blue door opened. She was standing there.

Hope walked out, glancing furtively from side to side, arms hugging her torso as her body hit the cold. She had on an oversized, cable-knit sweater, wool kneesocks, and clogs. She walked quickly over to Lucas.

"What the hell are you doing here?" Hope asked in a whisper.

"I . . . was . . . just . . ." Lucas inhaled. He was still winded from the run. "I had to see you."

Hope looked around again.

"What's wrong? Afraid someone is going to see us?" Lucas asked.

"What are you talking about?" Hope said.

"I thought maybe that was why you freaked out on me at school the other day."

"I did not freak out, Lucas," Hope said matter-of-factly. She grabbed the bottom of Lucas's zipped fleece running jacket and pulled hard, dragging him toward her.

"What are you doing?" Lucas asked, losing his balance.

"Well, you're here, aren't you? Wait. I have to get a key."

Lucas shook out his legs and leaned over to do a stretch. His quads and hamstrings felt tight. The cramp in his side still ached.

Hope reappeared in a blink with a set of keys in her hand.

"Let's go," she said, grabbing Lucas by the hand.

"Where?"

He followed her around the side of the house, where the snow had mostly melted, and down a ramp to a separate entrance, a basement door with a lock on the outside. Hope fit the key into the lock and turned on a light. Inside was a room like its own apartment, furnished with a small bathroom.

"Remember I told you about this place? My parents finally fixed it up to rent but no one has taken it yet," Hope said. "We might as well use it, right? Actually, I've been dying to come down here."

Lucas looked at her, with one eyebrow cocked as if to say, "Don't even try and convince me that you *haven't* been down here before with some other guy." Instead, he asked her, "Aren't your parents home?"

"My mom is sleeping upstairs. Dad's somewhere. I don't know."

Lucas briefly wondered why Hope's mother would be sleeping in the middle of a perfectly good day, even if it was just past February — what he considered to be the coldest month of the year. Lucas never understood how the shortest month always felt like the longest.

"What if your mom wakes up?"

"She won't. Earplugs," Hope said.

"Do you have something?" Lucas asked.

Hope nodded. She produced a package of condoms from one of the sweater pockets. "See? No problems." She reached up and wrapped her arms around Lucas's neck, but he pulled away.

"I'm all sweaty," he complained.

"I don't care about that," Hope said. "I like it."

She pulled his drenched running shirt up over his head. He undid the tie-waist on his pants and kicked off his sneakers. Hope let her sweater fall to the floor, revealing a silk camisole.

Lucas stroked the fabric. "Nice," he said, and then removed the camisole.

They grappled with the rest of Hope's clothes and then rolled onto the sofa bed stuck in the corner of the dark room. Lucas groped Hope's legs and she moaned like she liked it, poking her tongue into his ear. The room smelled of mothballs and the cushions were stiff with age. No one *had* really used this room for years. Lucas could tell. Maybe Hope hadn't been covering up. Maybe she hadn't brought other guys here.

Lucas decided he didn't care. He was the one here now. And Hope was on fire beneath him.

Outside the small room, Lucas heard the twitter of starlings or sparrows. He could hear a branch scraping along one of the shingles. And then there was the low rumble of a plane, and then another plane, flying high overhead.

Inside the room, Lucas heard the metronomelike ticking of an old 1960s alarm clock on a side table. Of course there was Hope, too, making all sorts of noises. She was touching him, touching herself. She rolled him over and got on top.

Lucas's body temperature escalated again, and he wondered whether he might actually be running a fever right now. This room was warmer than either of them expected it to be.

"I love body heat," Hope said, firmly planting her hands on his shoulders.

They moved together, their breathing synchronized. When it was over, Hope sat up and reached for a cigarette. "Do I have to go?" Lucas said. "I know it's late, but I don't want to. I don't want to leave you."

"I don't want you to leave me either," Hope said.

Looking up, Lucas noticed an area of peeling paint on the ceiling. Hope nestled in closer to him, tucking her head into his chest.

"I didn't tell you my big news today," Hope whispered. "I got one of the leads in the upcoming school play."

"You did what?" asked Lucas.

"I'm starring in *The Children's Hour* at school. How fabulous is that?"

"Fabulous," Lucas said, kissing the inside of her hand.

"The only drag is that I have to share the stage with Cady Sanchez."

"Why is that a drag?" Lucas asked seriously.

"I don't mean that *Cady* is a drag. I just . . . just . . ." Hope's voice faded. "I know she's your friend . . . and she'll be my friend, too, really she will, I'm sure of it. I just meant . . . I think maybe she was miscast. . . ."

"So she got a lead, too?" Lucas asked.

"Yes," Hope confirmed. "I have more lines, though."

Lucas smiled to himself. He'd pushed Cady so hard to audition, but it had paid off. He would call her the minute he got home to offer his congratulations.

"Lucas?" Hope asked, shoving Lucas in the side. "Are you *listening* to me?"

"Of course," Lucas said. "I heard you. You got all the lines."

He grabbed Hope's waist and rolled her over to face him. They started kissing again.

There was no better way than this to relax after such a long, strong run, Lucas thought. He and Hope had been great and then rocky but now things were really beginning to hit their stride.

He wished everyone on the Chesterfield soccer squad could see him like a peacock, feathers out, whenever he was with Hope. If only their relationship didn't have to be kept secret. Hope had wanted it that way from the beginning despite Lucas's complaints. Would she ever change her mind?

Lucas didn't care. He would make a song about this day, about this girl. He would make many songs, over and over, until his guitar strings snapped.

Slowly (and yes, surely), the love was coming back.

Chapter Nine

February 29, 1:00 PM
Cady

The weatherman said lots and lots of snow, and Cady knew he was right. She could always tell when it was just about to snow, when the vast sky turned crisp, steely blue, and the sycamores in her front yard seemed strangely, suddenly, more naked than ever before.

She pulled on her L. L. Bean waterproof moccasin boots, her brown cords, and her extra-large sweatshirt with BERKLEE COLLEGE OF MUSIC on the front. That was where she was headed for college next year, to study music and major in songwriting. Cady was excited to be heading to Boston's Back Bay for school, and since Lucas had lived there for his entire life, he had already told Cady about all the places she should visit. He'd made a lengthy list that included Quincy Market, the swan boats, Fenway's Green Monster, and even the Isabella Stewart Gardner Museum.

As she dressed, Cady imagined her future at college: afternoons composing in the park, feeding ducks, and baking in the sun during the warm months; ice skating and jamming in coffeehouses in Cambridge during the cold ones. Her parents had already scoped out the town, searching for studio apartments. They were pulling together their resources to make Cady's first year at college an A-plus. Diego was fond of saying that he was taking notes to make sure that he got the same special treatment when he went away to school.

Like almost every other senior at Chesterfield, Cady had reservations about leaving her small high school and the safety of the close-knit town. But Cady also knew she needed to move on, to grow and develop her musical talent. There was only so much growing that could happen at Big Cup gigs.

Deep down, Cady wished that Lucas would be a part of her journey to Berklee. Could he return to his old stomping grounds in Boston to show her around personally? Maybe he would even move back there? She'd encouraged him to apply, like her, but that seemed a losing battle. Lucas hardly ever talked about college. Even though he'd started Chesterfield as a B-plus student, he said that since the new year his grades had slipped to C-minuses and Ds and even a few Fs.

Cady had made plans today to head to the local art gallery, just to clear her head and get out of the house and chase away her winter blahs. She'd spent lots of her free time giving guitar lessons at Crestwood Music Center, but overall, the school break that week had been painfully boring. Marisol and Bebe had both skipped town with their extended families.

Cady pulled her heavy overcoat over her outfit, slipped on her wool hat and rainbow-colored mittens, and trudged outside. The air smelled cold. She inhaled deeply and started the long walk into town.

Upon arriving at the Prescott Art Gallery and walking

through the sterile marble lobby, Cady entered through a set of wide glass doors. It seemed at first that Cady had the gallery all to herself, until she realized that there were quite a few other visitors there, hiding out in the corners, gazing at the abstract sculptures and eighteenth-century oil paintings. It was an odd mix of mediums and masters, but it worked.

Cady stuffed her hands into the pockets of her cords and began a silent tour of the gallery. She stopped in front of one wall with the letters NEW ACQUISITIONS painted above a row of six giant canvases. Each one of the paintings was a view of the same harbor and field from a different perspective. One painting showed the view from a mountaintop. Another showed it from a dock. Still another showed a bird's-eye view from a passenger plane.

"Cady?"

Cady turned around when she heard her name. There was Lucas, iPod headphones on, dressed in running gear.

"What are you doing here?" Cady asked.

Lucas clicked off his iPod and shoved it into the pocket of his fleece. "I just came in here to warm up. Well, sort of. I wanted to see the sculptures, too. I saw one of these pieces over by The Woods once. Looked like a broken-down tractor with wings."

Cady nodded. "It's interesting."

"So," Lucas said. "You look good."

"I do?"

"Warm, anyway," Lucas said. "Nice sweatshirt."

Cady nodded. "Berklee sent me the packet of materials already. I can't believe I know where I'm going next year."

"That makes one of you," Lucas joked. "Half the guys on the soccer team are clueless. Some have actually applied to three reach schools and no safety schools. It's so out of whack."

"And what about you?" Cady asked.

"Still considering my options."

Lucas stepped to the side of Cady to look up at one of the enormous canvases.

"Man, these sure are big mothers," Lucas commented.

Cady looked up, too. "Yeah," she said. "Hey, do you want to check out those sculptures?"

Lucas liked that idea. They moved into the other main rooms of the gallery together.

"By the way," Lucas said, "Happy Leap Year."

"Still having a good vacation?" Cady asked.

"Sure," Lucas said. "A little boring, but you know how it is. I really liked getting together to play some music the other day, though. We should do more of it."

They strolled into a room filled with black-and-white photographs. Lucas coughed.

"Sorry," he mumbled, clearing his throat. "I've been sick on and off. Just a cold."

"Other than that, you're good?" Cady asked, trying to keep the conversation on its feet.

"Can't complain," Lucas said. The wide smile on his face piqued Cady's curiosity.

"What's with the grin?" Cady asked.

"Nothing," Lucas said. "I've been getting a lot of exercise. You know. Those endorphins kick in and wham, I'm in good shape."

"I wish. I've been nothing but a slug this winter," Cady admitted. "I should try to lose a few pounds before the summer."

"Lose it from where?" Lucas asked, sizing up Cady's body with disbelief. "You're perfect."

"Thanks for that vote of confidence," Cady replied, trying to sound breezy, but loving the compliment.

They shuffled around the gallery room and then headed back to the lobby. Lucas said he wanted to finish his run. He jumped up and down in place. "My calves are getting a little stiff in here. I'm going to have to go back out," he said, stretching out his arms so wide that he nearly knocked right into a sculpture entitled *Woman with Can.*

The gallery security guard gave Lucas a suspicious look.

"Now *that* dude would make a great partner for *Woman with Can,*" Lucas joked, referring to the guard.

Cady stifled a little laugh. "There are odder couples in the world," she mused aloud. "Take my parents, for example."

"Where is your dad from again?"

"Colombia."

"Ever been there?"

"Nope." Cady shook her head. "Dad doesn't want to go back. I told him I'll go see my *abuelita* someday. I hope I do."

"Where did your parents meet?"

"On a plane. Mom was a flight attendant."

"So he picked her up, huh?" Lucas said with a laugh.

"I guess. And once they started seeing each other, he decided to give up everything in his country to move closer to my mom. That's when they got engaged and then they moved here to Chesterfield. Pretty random."

"No more random than anyone else's life, I guess," Lucas said.

Cady watched Lucas stare off into space. She guessed that he was probably thinking about his own parents, about his own mother. He seemed to do that whenever the subject of family came up.

"Lucas, are you okay?" Cady asked.

"I am. And I'm really glad I ran into you," Lucas said. "You know how to make me smile."

"Me?" Cady asked, caught off guard.

"Yeah, you. You're real good at making people happy. I wish I'd met you before New Year's."

Lucas turned away, and as he did, Cady noticed a scar she hadn't seen before, just over his left eye. She reached up gently to touch it.

"Where is this one from?" Cady asked.

"You don't want to know. I slammed into a door. Like I always say, every scar has a story. But that doesn't necessarily mean that the story is going to be interesting."

"Looks like it was deep," Cady said. She stroked his eyebrow with her fingertip, holding his gaze steady. "That must have hurt."

"Yes," Lucas said, his voice getting lower. "They all hurt."

He'd been racing to get out of there, but Cady saw that with the slightest touch he was fixed to the ground. His running shoes held him in place. For that very brief moment, *she* held him in place.

"Well," Lucas said, as if coming to. "I really do have to run."

Cady laughed. "I know, I know. See you in school?"

Lucas nodded as he hustled back toward the gallery exit, stopping once to lean over and retie his sneaker.

Cady roamed around the gallery for a while longer, passing the photographs and even the little room packed with dark oil paintings from the 1700s. She circled back around *Woman with Can*, smiling at the day's happy coincidence. Then she grabbed her coat, hat, and mittens, and headed outside.

The snow was coming down fast and wet like white rain. From the look of it, there was already more than an inch on the ground. Cady briefly considered calling her mom or dad to come and pick her up, but decided against it. She would walk all the way back home. Her waterproof boots would get her there.

The sidewalks were slippery, and Cady wondered where Lucas had run off to, with his hood pulled snug around his face. She loved the idea of him running through the snowstorm, feet crunching the ice and salt on the roads, little icicles forming on his jacket. His movements were a song cutting through the winter wind.

And the truth was that Lucas Wheeler didn't just move like music.

He was music. Cady's music.

Chapter Eight

February 22, 12:20 PM
Hope

"You're so tanned!" Lenora cried when she saw Hope.

Hope groaned. She'd worked hard on the tan, but she didn't want anyone to know that. Although everyone who was anyone used regular tanning salon appointments to keep their skin looking golden pink during the winter months, there was still *nothing* like a genuine beach tan. Hope didn't think about the cancer risk from baking in the hot Paradise Island sun. She thought about the look, her look, and she had to look good. It was a part of who she was.

Hope had agreed to meet her friends Pam and Lenora at Zen Living, a juice bar in downtown Chesterfield, once she'd gotten back from her trip. It was a vacation that started in Florida and moved progressively south, ending up in the Bahamas. Her parents had brought Hope and her sisters, Haylie and Hannah, along for a winter extrava-ganza. Every year they planned one. This was not a family who liked to hang out at home with each other. This was a family who looked for the next great resort. Sometimes Hope wondered if she was missing out on the sentimental parts of life, but she had decided long ago that seeing the world, shopping, and sun-worshipping usually made up for that. Usually.

Of course she'd missed Lucas, just a little bit, as much

as she didn't want to admit it. The entire time she'd been away, Hope had kept him in the back of her thoughts.

Lenora waved her hand in the air, showing off her latest sparkling prize. On her right hand, fourth finger, she proudly displayed a yellow stone.

"Looks like a diamond, right?" Lenora boasted.

Hope didn't think it looked much like a diamond at all.

"Where did you get that? Box of Frosted Flakes?" Hope cracked.

Lenora frowned. "What did you say? Oh my *God*." She feigned utter disgust.

Pam, their other friend, laughed gingerly. "Oh, Hopie, you're just kidding, right?"

Hope rolled her eyes. "Yes, of course I'm kidding," she said.

Lately, something had been off between Hope and her girlfriends, and she wasn't sure what. Part of the problem was college applications. Hope's first pick was Stanford, and her 3.9 GPA, high SAT scores, extracurriculars, and Daddy's money just about assured her acceptance. Lenora and Pam would have killed to go to a college like that, but they didn't have the same grades or clout that Hope did. Not that Stanford was the be all and end all, Hope thought. But it just seemed like the best, and Hope wanted nothing but the best—especially if she could get a tan at the same time.

Hope's friends chatted about their winter break holidays. They compared party notes: best outfits, best drinks, cutest guys. Hope joined in the talk by making up some story about fooling around with two guys in one night on Paradise Island. Lenora and Pam ate it up. They blindly believed whatever Hope said. Of course, they knew nothing about Lucas Wheeler, but that was the way Hope wanted it.

Both Pam and Lenora would have traded their best pair of Jimmy Choo knockoffs to get it on with Lucas. Not only had the school paper named Lucas the hottest new kid back when senior year had started, but as the year continued, the "Lucas mystique" had continued to grow. Word on the street (though no one knew where the word had come from) was that Lucas Wheeler was good in bed.

Hope chuckled to herself when she thought about it. She had managed to get so many rumors out there without anyone, not even Cady Sanchez, knowing that Hope was the crash-test dummy. But she loved nothing more than knowing that she and she alone possessed this one person everyone else desired. Lucas was Hope's source of power these days, whether or not she felt like seeing him.

It had been nearly a week since Hope and Lucas had hooked up last, so part of missing him was purely a physical thing. Somewhere in the middle of the chat with Lenora and Pam, Hope decided that she was going to pay Lucas a surprise visit. She knew his dad wasn't home. And even if he was home, he didn't care. She knew a lot of things about the Wheeler family, things that helped her to get everything she wanted, or at least most of the things she wanted.

Hope hated driving on icy roads, but, after saying goodbye to her friends, she got into her car and motored over to Lucas's house. The driveway was empty. For a moment,

Hope wondered if even Lucas was home, but then she caught a glimpse of his car, top up, in the garage.

She wrapped her peacoat tight against herself as she walked up the stairway toward his front door. It was covered with vines bunched in icy, brown clumps. *This yard needs so much work*, Hope thought as she tripped up the brick steps to the front landing. She didn't understand how Lucas's dad could let things get into such a state of disrepair when he could just write a check and have everything fixed *for* him.

When she opened the glass storm door to knock, the scent of pine filled Hope's nose. She was surprised to see a giant Christmas wreath still hanging there, decorated with pinecones that had long since dried out. It took at least three minutes before Hope heard the click in the lock and the door opened.

"Surprise!" Hope cried, arms over her head. "I'm back."

Lucas rubbed his eyes. "I was sleeping," he mumbled. He walked back inside, leaving the door open.

"Is your father home?" Hope asked, sounding polite, just in case.

"No," Lucas said. "Close the door when you come in."

Hope stepped inside, kicked off her wet boots, and slammed the door shut.

"Let's go down to the basement," Lucas said, sniffling.

"Are you sick?" Hope asked as they went downstairs.

Lucas coughed. "Flu. You might want to stay away." He hacked into his closed fist, a hard, brutal cough that sounded as if it might never go away.

"What stinks?" Hope said, trying to get comfortable on the sofa down in Lucas's basement.

"It's the litter," Lucas said. "The cats are upstairs."

Hope reached out to pet Boo Radley, Lucas's dog, but Boo wasn't cooperating. He growled at her, showing teeth.

"Boo!" Lucas scolded. "Get back," he added, tugging on Boo's tough leather collar.

"I didn't do anything," Hope whined as Lucas pulled the dog away. "You know, he smells worse than the cat litter."

Boo growled and Lucas stroked the top of his head. The dog always got so jumpy when Hope came around. She knew part of it was a mix of jealousy and protectiveness for Lucas. Hope hated how Lucas always told her how much he enjoyed having a pet that was so completely loyal, more loyal than anyone or anything in his life had ever been.

Hope wanted to show Lucas a thing or two about loyalty.

She leaned back on the sofa. "Did you have a nice break?" she asked.

"You were supposed to call me," Lucas said.

"Was I?" Hope put on a face like she was thinking. "I forgot."

"You didn't forget the tanning oil, though, did you?"

"You like?" Hope asked, posing as if she were on a photo shoot for Hawaiian Tropic.

"Weren't you supposed to be coming back to Chesterfield a few days ago?"

"Plans change. Sorry. Did you miss me?"

Lucas stood up to blow his nose. He threw the used tissue into a basket right next to Hope. She could tell how angry he was.

"You need a drink?" Lucas asked.

"Yeah, vodka," Hope said.

"Um . . . not in this house," Lucas said. His father had been in AA for more than a year, and the house was as dry as a bone.

"No kidding," Hope snarled. She always complained that she could never do anything fun (like drink) when she and Lucas hung out at his place. But that was the price she'd agreed to pay when she decided to keep their relationship so hush-hush.

"I'll run upstairs and get you a Coke," Lucas said.

"Diet. You know I don't drink sugar soda," Hope said.

"I'll get you a glass of water then."

"With ice."

Lucas went to get the drinks. Hope stood before the three photographs on the wall.

"I think I really captured the real you in these shots," she said smugly, staring at the photos when Lucas returned.

Lucas handed her the cup. "I think you know a lot about the real me," Lucas said.

"I had you figured out the night we met," Hope said.

Lucas reached out for her waist. "So, what's your poison?" he teased, grabbing her and pulling her close.

She pushed him away. "Not here. It smells down here."

"It's no different than any of the other times," Lucas said.

"Only now you have the flu, remember?"

"Right."

Lucas collapsed onto the sofa by himself.

"So what did you do this week in Paradise?" Lucas asked.

"Hmmm. Let me see. Drank more than a few shots. Met some guys on the beach. Danced until three or four every night. It was great. The Bahamas are the best. Even my two sisters partied with me. What about you?" Hope asked. "What did you do?"

"Spent a lot of time alone," he said. "Went for runs. Waited by the phone."

"Oh, Lucas," Hope said, leaning in closer. "I did think about you — about us — when I was away."

Lucas continued as if he hadn't heard her. "I went away with Dad and Aunt Rita, played some music with Cady."

"Cady?" Hope said.

"Yeah, she came over one day. We're working on this song."

"Wait." Hope felt her claws extend. "You spent a day — *here* — with Cady Sanchez?"

"Yeah. Dad was in and out. We played a pickup game out back. That was funny."

"Touch football?"

Lucas laughed. "Yeah. She and I like a lot of the same things, actually."

"You said you wouldn't see other people. We agreed."

"Hold up. It's not like that." Lucas shook his head. He sneezed and coughed, rubbed the raw tip of his swollen nose.

"What about us?"

"*Us?*" Lucas asked, sounding incredulous. "You won't

even be seen in public with me. And you're the one who just went to the Bahamas, for chrissakes. Anyway, Cady and I are just friends. Good friends. She's nice."

"Nice?" Hope snickered.

"What's the matter with nice?"

"You need to stop talking to her," Hope said. "Or you're going to give her the wrong idea."

"What do you care?" Lucas asked. He tried to put his arm around Hope, but she moved away.

"Just do what I tell you," Hope said.

"Come on, Hope. I can't just stop talking to Cady," Lucas said. "Believe me, she doesn't have the wrong idea."

Hope picked up Lucas's guitar and held it out in front of her.

"What are you doing?" he asked.

"I said I want you to stop seeing her."

Hope looked him square in the eye. "You write songs with her. You don't write me songs," she declared, her hands around the neck of the guitar like she was choking it.

Lucas made a face. "I do write you songs," he said. "I just wrote that one for Valentine's Day."

"I know what this is all *really* about," Hope said. "You had sex with Cady, didn't you?"

"Whoa," Lucas cried. "What are you talking about?"

"Answer the question."

"I don't need this. I'm sick, remember?"

"You're sick? I'm the one who is sick here. I could have been with a dozen or more guys in the Bahamas, but I saved myself for you."

"You what? You saved yourself? You're kidding, right?"

Hope raised her hand and slapped Lucas right across his cheek.

He recoiled. "What the hell was that?" Lucas asked, eyes wide open with surprise.

She raised her hand and slapped him again on the other cheek. This time, Lucas grabbed her wrist.

"Hey. Tiger," Lucas said. He coughed. "Don't do that again, okay? It really hurt."

"Why are you lying to me?" Hope said, disintegrating into tears.

"Hope, stop this," Lucas pleaded.

Hope cried even louder. "You can't *treat* me this way, Lucas!" she wailed.

"Treat you what way?"

"I can't . . . I won't . . ." Now she was hysterical.

"Hope!" Lucas grabbed her again. "Stop crying. Please stop crying."

"Don't you understand? I don't want anyone else to have you," Hope whimpered.

Lucas sighed. "I know," he said.

Hope sat there for a few moments, sobbing quietly.

"You're mine, Lucas."

"I know," Lucas said, his own voice softening.

Hope looked right into his eyes and reached for his belt. "Take off your pants," she ordered.

"Um, Hope." Lucas coughed. "I'm not exactly in the mood. . . ."

"What's the matter? I don't look good enough for you?" Hope asked. "Not as good as Cady?"

"Come on. You look fantastic," Lucas said. "You look

like a berry all sun-kissed like that. And the white shirt shows it off. Nice."

"Nice. Yeah. That word again."

"Relax, please."

"Don't tell me what to do!" Hope cried, spitting the words.

"Hope . . ."

"Leave me alone!" Hope yelled.

As Hope angrily pulled away from Lucas, she swung her arm wide, out to the side. There was a picture there. She saw it. But she knocked it off the wall anyway.

A green-framed shot of Lucas's mother, taken at the beach, crashed to the floor.

Lucas reeled backward. He bent down to pick up the frame, but before he could grab it, Hope raced over and kicked it. The frame slid into the wall and cracked at the corner. But that wasn't enough. Hope was still seething. She grabbed the cup of water that Lucas had brought downstairs and hurled that glass against the wall. Lucas cried out as it flew into an antique mirror instead. A corner piece of the mirror shattered.

"What the hell did you do that for?" Lucas shouted.

From the other room, Boo began to bark.

"Shut up, Boo!" Lucas yelled. He ran his hand through the top of his hair, looking frantic. Calmly, Hope sat down on the sofa. "You shouldn't have gotten such a cheap frame," she said, crossing her legs.

"Why did you *do that*?" Lucas said, voice taut as a wire. "That was my mother's."

"Your mother's?" Hope replied. "So?"

"So it means something to me."

"Lucas, I don't want to upset you or anything, but you have this strange mother-thing going on," Hope said in a calculated tone. "I mean, what *is* this? Some kind of shrine to her?" She gestured around the room in disgust.

"Shrine?" Lucas's jaw dropped. "She was my mother, Hope. I miss her."

"I know. But she died," Hope said. "She's gone, Lucas. Deal."

Lucas started to say something, but the words seemed to stick in his throat.

"You need to get over it already, Lucas. It's been what — two years?" Hope sighed. "That's a long time."

A stillness in the air between them blocked sound like a sheet of plastic wrap.

Lucas collapsed onto the sofa next to Hope. His eyes flooded with a stream of tears.

"Shhh," Hope said. She stroked the side of his face. "I know it's hard. But everyone loses someone. You just have to move on. It's time."

"Time?" Lucas wiped his eyes. "Shit! What time is it?" he asked, still sniffing.

"I don't know." Hope pointed to the VCR/DVD. The time flashed digital blue.

"I'm late."

"Late for what?" Hope asked.

"Dr. Shakely," Lucas said. "I already missed last week's session when we blew off school to see that movie in the middle of the day."

"Oh Lucas, you don't need a doctor," Hope smiled.

"You have me." Lucas caught his breath. He looked right at Hope. She could feel his eyes soften. It was working. "Blow off your doctor," Hope said, keeping her gaze steady. "I mean, what's more important than right now?"

She unlatched the button at the top of her skirt.

Within moments, the two of them fell back on the sofa, cat stink, barking Boo, and all.

Chapter Seven

February 14, 11:41 PM
Lucas

"I can't believe we're doing this," Lucas said, laughing to himself.

"You never know until you try," Hope said.

It was nearly midnight. They walked up and down behind the Tremont Bakery warehouse, behind the line of deserted bread trucks. The full moon played tricks on Lucas's eyes. It cast shadows that looked like ghosts, or what he imagined ghosts might look like: tiny, dark wisps that appeared and disappeared with the breeze.

Hope pulled a pack of cigarettes out of her handbag.

"Want one?" Hope asked, offering Lucas a cigarette.

Lucas took the cigarette and then broke it in half.

"Hey!" Hope snapped. "That cigarette cost like a buck."

Lucas made a face. "A buck? Quit before you're broke."

Hope pulled out another one and lit up. "Fat chance," she said, taking a deep drag and blowing the smoke right back out in Lucas's face.

Lucas walked back and forth, jimmying the trucks' back doors. The first one was locked. Then he tried another one and then another one.

It was cold out here. He blew into his hands.

Tremont Bakery was located up on a hilltop overlooking Chesterfield, all 1.56 square miles of it. White, gold, blue, and orange lights flickered in the distance. Everyone seemed so far away from here. The bakery had an alarm system on the store, but fortunately no security guard patrolling the parking lot. Hope had suggested they get together someplace new and different on Valentine's Day. When she mentioned the bakery, Lucas got the distinct feeling she'd been there before.

"Try that door," Hope suggested, pointing to a truck with a splatter of blue paint on the back.

Lucas tried. It was unlocked.

Hope tossed her cigarette butt, and it rolled under the back wheels. The metal door clanged and shook as Lucas lifted it and climbed up into the back of the truck, trying hard not to knock his arm or head into the rows of metal shelves.

Everything smelled like bread.

"Here's your sleeping bag," Hope said, tossing it up into the back of the truck.

Lucas lifted it—and her—inside. She let out a howl of joy.

"What are you doing? Someone might hear," he said.

Hope laughed. "Who cares?"

"How much did you have to drink again?"

Hope playfully smacked his face. "None of your beeswax," she said, laughing. "How much did *you* have?"

Lucas unzipped the sleeping bag. Hope gasped when she looked down. Rose petals were everywhere.

"What is this?" Hope asked.

"You said you like roses. So, Happy Valentine's Day," Lucas said. "And I have something else for you, too."

Hope settled back on the petals. "What else?" she asked.

Lucas clapped his hand against the side of the bread truck to keep time. He began to sing.

Suppose I said there's no good reason
For the snow or the sea
Or even me
But here we go anyway
Two of a kind and
Now I find
My way home again
When I'm with you
I can do what I've wanted to
For a lifetime
My sweet, sweet Valentine

Lucas stopped, humming the tune a second time, repeating only the last line. He was trying to read Hope's expression. What was she thinking?

"That's so . . . hot," Hope said, licking her lips. She grabbed his collar and pulled them both down, mouths open. Clumsily they tugged off coats and then sweaters and climbed into the bag. Lucas saw little bumps all along his forearm, making the hairs stand up.

"Cold?" Hope asked. She brushed the petals out of the way and moved on top of him. Slowly, she tickled her fingers along his belly, stopping short on a nub of scarred skin.

"Barbecue accident," Lucas said quickly, pushing her hand away.

"You can get your scars removed, you know," Hope said. "That's why they have plastic surgery."

"Why would I get them removed?" Lucas asked, blinking. Hope's hands moved lower. How did she keep them so warm in here?

"Lucas," Hope purred his name. "Tell me what you're thinking."

"Actually, I'm not thinking," Lucas said, smiling.

"This place is really deserted," Hope said, lying down on her side, pressed up close to Lucas. "I'm surprised. Usually all the stoners come up to Tremont to smoke."

"No one else is here because everyone knew we had it reserved," Lucas said.

"What are you talking about, 'everyone knew'?" Hope said.

"I was kidding," Lucas said.

Hope stood up and exhaled a fancy smoke ring right at Lucas's head. She threw on her pants and sweater.

"I have to piss," Hope said, giggling as she slipped on her cowboy boots.

"Here?"

"No, outside. I'll be right back," Hope said. "Open the door for me."

Lucas lifted it up and she jumped out.

After she'd gone, he leaned over and pulled out a pen and a worn composition notebook from his bag. He removed an oversized rubber band, shuffled a few of the papers that were stuffed inside, and opened to a clean page near the back. Lately, he had to write down thoughts as soon as they came into his head or else they might vanish forever. Besides, it could be good material for a song.

Here we are. Bread truck. Shit!!! And I sang her the song. She liked it. I think. Together four weeks and I feel like this new person. Hope White makes Chesterfield work for me. I've been spending time with Cady and she's cute, too, but different. I think Hope is more my speed. What would Frank say about all this? He'd say what the hell are you doing in a freaking bread truck? That's what he'd say. Ha. I miss him and his dumb-ass jokes. I miss Molly, too. She e-mailed me last week and I never even wrote back. I can just hear her whining what's your problem Luke? I hated when she called me that. But now I miss it. I miss

"What *is* that?" Hope's eyelashes fluttered as she poked her head back into the truck.

Lucas pulled the journal back and rewrapped the rubber band. "Nothing," he said.

"No. Let me see," Hope said, climbing on top of him. "Read me a page."

Lucas grinned and held the book just out of reach. "This is my personal shit. I can't just read it to you."

"Why not?" Hope asked, batting her lashes. "It's just me. Don't you want to share everything with me? Besides, what are you doing writing in a notebook in the middle of our date?"

Lucas chuckled. "It's just something I do," he said, clutching the notebook closer to his chest. With one hand he shoved the book back into the bag. With the other hand he pulled out two ice-cold beers.

"I really wish . . ." Lucas started to say.

"What?" Hope asked, twisting off the cap of her beer.

"I just wish . . . we could tell everyone, you know?" Lucas continued. "That we're dating. I wish I could tell everyone that you, Hope White, are my girlfriend."

"Your girlfriend?" Hope said. "Hold up, cowboy."

"What do you mean, 'hold up'?" Lucas asked.

"I'm not really into labels, Lucas. I think it's better if we just keep this between us, like I said when we first got together."

"Okay. I guess I can live with that."

"Good," Hope said, kissing his cheek. She swigged the beer.

"What am I gonna do without you for a whole week?" Lucas asked.

"Lose your mind," Hope teased. "What else?"

Lucas's finger traced her lips. "Being with you is almost perfect, Hope, do you know that? It's like poetry and music, and sometimes I find myself thinking about your hair, your face, your —"

"I get the picture," Hope said.

"What kind of music do you like?" Lucas asked, fumbling with the sleeping bag. For some reason, his legs were freezing. The zipper had gotten stuck.

"Music? Oh, I don't know. I don't really care," Hope replied.

184

"How can you not care about music?"

"Because other things are more important." Hope reached out for his neck and pulled him toward her, poking her tongue into his ear — just a little. "There's music for your ears."

"Mmm," Lucas murmured. "You're such a romantic."

Lucas slid his hand across Hope's shoulder blades and down her spine, stopping at each vertebra. Outside, the winter wind blew, and the chill filled the back of the truck, even with the door shut.

Hope and Lucas pushed together again like a sandwich.

"Hope, how come you never talk about your family?" Lucas murmured. He didn't know why he'd asked the question. He just wanted to know.

Hope looked confused. "Mom's a mom and my stepdad's a banker. You met my sisters. Blond One and Blond Two. My family is beyond boring."

"But what about your real dad?"

"You mean my biological father?"

Lucas nodded.

"He's around. Look, can we talk about something else? I'm really not very complicated. I swear. And it's Valentine's Day. . . ."

Lucas laughed. "Yeah, sure, sorry," he said with a little snort. All at once, his phone rang out: an escalating, vibrating scale.

Hope glanced at her watch. "Who is calling you after midnight on Valentine's Day?"

"I don't know," Lucas said with a shrug. He leaned

down and snatched up the phone from the pocket of his jeans. "It must be important. Hello?"

Lucas turned away from Hope to talk, but she grabbed his shoulder, pulling him back.

"Um . . . I can't talk now," Lucas mumbled into the receiver. He clicked the cell off.

"Who *was* that?" Hope said out loud, very loud.

Lucas shoved the phone back into his pocket. "No one."

"No one?" Hope crossed her arms in front. "Lucas, tell me who that was."

"It was just Cady. No biggie. She had a question—"

"Cady? Had a question? At midnight on Valentine's Day? You must be joking."

"Nah. She seemed a little bummed today, so I told her that she could call me whenever," Lucas said, trying to play it cool. "She's working on a song and had some trouble with one of the chords. . . ."

"You're an asshole."

Hope sat up and buttoned her sweater and coat.

Lucas sat there, a little stunned, still half-naked under the sleeping bag.

"What? You're going?" he asked.

Hope threw her head back and popped another cigarette into her mouth. She tried to open the back of the truck with one hand, but it was too heavy.

"Wait. Don't go," Lucas said. "I didn't know Cady would call. I didn't know."

Hope turned and looked at Lucas, hard.

"You really didn't know?"

Lucas nodded. "I promise."

186

"Don't ever lie to me," Hope said coldly. "I mean it. This better not happen again."

"Don't worry," Lucas said gently. He reached up and guided Hope back under the blankets. She was reluctant at first but then she kicked her shoes off and climbed in. "Aahh!" Lucas twisted to the side. "Your feet are like ice."

"So warm me up," Hope purred. Lucas pulled the blankets tighter around them.

In so many places in his life Lucas was looking— desperately— for a second chance.

For now, Lucas was convinced that Hope was the one who would give it to him.

Chapter Six

February 14, 4:00 PM
Cady

Mr. Drake had been teaching music at Chesterfield High School for his entire career: thirty-nine long (and he said happy) years. Cady didn't understand how someone could stay in one place for nine years, let alone *thirty-nine* years. It sounded like the job equivalent of shackling yourself to a radiator.

But what Mr. Drake lacked in terms of traveling around, he made up for in consistency, musical ear, and a genuine fondness for the students in his classes. He'd been the inspiration for numerous Chesterfield kids who had gone on to successful careers in music and music production. Everyone always joked that he was like Mr. Holland in the flick *Mr. Holland's Opus*, only he didn't have a wife or a deaf kid. Mr. Drake was *all* about the music. He'd been the one person who had pushed Cady to apply to Berklee even when she doubted her chances of acceptance. He'd written her a glowing letter of recommendation and got the Big Cup owner to do the same.

From the moment Lucas arrived at Chesterfield, Mr. Drake had sensed Lucas's musical talent, too. He'd brought Lucas in to work on all their music projects. That was the first place Cady had seen Lucas up close, before they'd officially met at the New Year's party. Lucas didn't know, however, that Cady had watched him through the window of Mr. Drake's classroom, ogling the new kid not for his good looks, but for the way his fingers moved along the frets of his guitar. She had wondered many times what those calloused tips would feel like touching the back of her neck.

In a way, Mr. Drake had been their true matchmaker.

And here she was, just weeks later, no longer a spy. Cady and Lucas sat side by side in Mr. Drake's music classroom, long after class had ended and the teacher had gone, practicing chords from one of Lucas's original songs. He'd made up the melody but it had no words. He was looking for inspiration.

"I suck at the poetry parts," Lucas said.

Cady disagreed. "Everything you do in here is like poetry. What are you talking about?"

"You flatter me," Lucas said, turning back to his guitar.

"Well," Cady said, giggling. "Maybe."

Cady thought she saw Lucas blush, although she couldn't be sure. Sometimes his skin looked ruddy, especially under the fluorescent lights inside the school building.

"Your songs, at least the ones you shared in class, all have this flow," Lucas mumbled. "I can't make words make sense like you can. I need a translator."

"We should try playing a song together," Cady suggested.

"Well, I guess it's better than playing with myself," Lucas said.

Cady's eyes got wide and she giggled. Lucas realized what he'd said.

"Oh, God. You know what I meant, right?" Lucas asked.

"You ever think about playing at Big Cup?" Cady said, changing the subject.

"That's the place downtown, right? The café or whatever?"

Cady nodded. "You'd be perfect. You could have all the girls swooning."

Lucas grinned. "Jesus. I'm going to get a big head if you don't watch out."

Cady laughed again, nervously. She felt her face turn beet-red. "And you say you're no good with words?" she teased.

"God!" Lucas said, rolling his eyes. "I can't believe I said that either."

Cady looked away, a little embarrassed because Lucas was making all these unconscious, funny double entendres. But she didn't mind. In his own way, Lucas was so disarmingly genuine. Cady knew, despite all appearances, Lucas *didn't* have a big ego.

He was just as lost as the rest of the world.

"Cady, let me ask you something," Lucas said. "What does music do for you?"

Cady paused, thinking.

"Stumped you, huh?" Lucas asked. "Because it wasn't a hard question."

"No, it is a hard question," Cady said. "For some reason . . ."

A silence lingered between them for a moment. Twenty or thirty seconds passed, and their eyes stayed locked but no words escaped. Cady felt a swirl, a twitch inside of her as they stared.

Just who *was* this guy?

"That's it, isn't it?" Lucas said.

"What's it?" Cady asked, fearful for a moment that he could read her thoughts.

"The quiet, the silence. *That's* what music is really about," Lucas said.

Cady laughed. "I'm not sure I understand."

"Some music, crap music, is just noise, you know? But music that speaks to us is about each note, each rest, each moment filling the silence and letting the silence just be. Really good music is about the notes and the silence in between the notes."

Cady wasn't sure she understood completely what Lucas was talking about, but then again, he could have been reciting the Yellow Pages. She just loved to hear him speak, the way he dropped his voice at the end of each sentence almost like a growl, like a rock star.

"Writing music is about taking the silence seriously. It's about letting it be, like in Beethoven's Fifth when those first four notes play and then . . . nothing."

"Did Mr. Drake or some other music teacher tell you this?" Cady asked.

"Nah, I just think about this stuff a lot. Don't you?"

Lucas looked back down at his guitar for a moment, and Cady became acutely aware of the silence, his silence.

"I always thought music was a little like meditation," Cady said.

Lucas looked up at her and Cady felt her stomach flip. His eyes were so beautiful, like chestnuts flecked with gold.

"Meditation?" Lucas said. "See? You understand exactly where I'm coming from. *Exactly.*"

"Maybe," Cady said, her voice a little wobbly. She'd never talked to any boy in her class who seemed so soulful, so full.

"Music is there for us sometimes when nothing else or no one else is there," Lucas went on.

He launched into some jazz chords on his guitar, singing in a low voice, a little off-key and raspy, but filled with edgy tones that could make a song work.

I feel the sound, the pound, around
Come to me like the sea
Emily
Only you can set me free

"*That's* sort of poetic," Cady said dazedly. It was rough and it rhymed too much, but she liked it. "Who's Emily?"

"I don't know. It sounded good. It rhymed. My girl-friend at the time was Rebecca. Nothing rhymed with that. Dumb, right?"

"No, it's good," Cady said again, feeling an inexplicable twinge of jealousy.

"You know, music is the oldest religious rite we have," Lucas said, going philosophical. "Our ancestors sang songs to pray. They used rhythm and music to make sense of things. How did the universe work? Music gave answers or a way to express the answers."

If someone had taken a candid photograph of Cady watching Lucas speak, the image would have captured her dumbfounded, slack-jawed expression. The school paper had called Lucas the number one "hottie" in school, but Cady was pretty sure that no one else in Chesterfield knew about this side of Lucas, the musical, thoughtful side. Was he showing her his private self for a reason? Did he have the same intuition as Cady about what connected them — or what could connect them? Was there a way to describe this boy to anyone without having one of her friends break out into disabling laughter? Guys like Lucas did not exist; certainly not at this high school. They only existed in romance novels — or deep inside Cady's imagination.

But Cady believed.

She saw the potential for their relationship laid out in front of her like a musical composition: quarter, half, and whole notes trilling along until the coda and refrain. She thought about the journal she'd kept for half her life, with song ideas and personal dramas recounted for posterity. Lucas was the "guy" she'd always dreamed and written about, right down to his cowlick. From the moment they had met at the party, she'd had an idea that he was the one, but now she was convinced.

"Have you ever written a song about someone and captured that person exactly the way you wanted?" Lucas asked.

Cady blinked. "I tried," she said. "Once, I almost did. I wrote about this boy I liked."

"Ah, the jilted lover song," Lucas said.

"Well, not lover exactly," Cady said.

"Oh, sorry," Lucas said. "I just assumed."

All at once, Cady felt her skin pale. She put her hand on her own neck and felt for a pulse. He'd assumed what? That she'd had sex? It wasn't a crazy thing. As far as Cady knew, at least three-quarters of the girls in her senior class had had sex.

"You shouldn't assume, I guess," Cady said.

"Yeah, I know. ASS out of U and ME and all. I just figured that someone like you . . ." Lucas trailed off.

"Like me?"

"You dating anyone now?" Lucas asked. It was an obvious follow-up.

"No, I'm not . . . now . . ." she said, a little defensive, a lot embarrassed. "You know I'm not. What about you, Mr. Mysterious?"

"I'm the new kid, remember?" Lucas quipped.

"Every girl in class would hook up with you if you gave them a chance," Cady said, feeling reckless.

"*Every* girl?" Lucas laughed. He glanced up at the clock in the music room. It was closing in on five o'clock. "It's late," he muttered, packing his guitar away in his case.

Cady put her guitar away, too, tried to switch gears. "Um . . . you have plans for Valentine's Day?" Cady asked.

Lucas shook his head. "Not really."

"The only reason I ask is because if you don't have anything going on," Cady said, "I'm going to Big Cup for an open mic—"

"Wow," Lucas said.

"Yeah," Cady said, a little breathless. "So if you want to come . . ."

"I can't," Lucas said plainly.

"Oh." Cady sighed. "So you do have plans. Well, that's okay," she said, even though she felt that it was most decidedly *not* okay.

"Why don't you ask someone else to go with you?" Lucas suggested.

"There is no one else," Cady said without realizing it.

For a fleeting moment, the silence came back—loud. Cady looked away. Maybe she'd been wrong. Maybe her instincts that they had been so much alike were wrong. Maybe Cady wasn't anything like Lucas's type. Maybe it was time to give up on guys. Right now Cady was just about ready to give up on everything, including guitar.

Lucas packed up his things and zipped his soft guitar case.

"It's funny. At my old school in Massachusetts, I was friends with everyone. But I never knew a girl quite like you," Lucas said.

Cady wasn't sure if Lucas meant that in a good way.

"So we should get together again soon," Lucas said.

"Yeah," Cady said numbly. "Soon."

"You know, you can call me anytime," Lucas said.

"Okay. I will."

"I wish I'd found a songwriting friend like you before the middle of the year," he added, strapping his guitar to his back.

The word "friend" echoed inside Cady's head.

Friend. Friend. Friend.

Of course. That was it, wasn't it? She had to accept it.

But it would be so hard. Cady felt like there was a neon orange NO VACANCY sign flashing in her head, because whether he knew it or not, Lucas had moved right in. He'd been inside there since the night on the couch at Emile's party.

And Cady had no idea how to get him out.

Chapter Five

Paddy's Diner was packed. The parrot cage was decorated with tinsel and colored bulbs that had been up since before Christmas.

Hope stuck her foot out under the booth where she sat with Lucas and slid off her shoe. She slowly ran her toes up the seam of his jeans.

Lucas jerked forward. "Hope!" he cried, surprised. He pushed her foot away. "Not here," he said.

"Why not?" Hope asked, leaning across the table to grab his hands. "We've been doing it everywhere else."

Lucas brushed his hair off his face and leaned forward to meet her halfway. "Because," he whispered, "I'm saving myself."

Hope leaned back and laughed out loud. "I don't know *what* you're saving," she teased. "You're mine, Wheeler."

"Wait!" Lucas's eyes lit up. "Hold that thought!" he said. "I just got an idea."

Hope sat back, intrigued. "What kind of idea?"

"I . . . can't . . . tell you," Lucas said in a singsong voice. "The only thing is, I have to run out for just a minute. Can you wait for me to get back?"

"Sure, I guess. Hey, where are you going?"

"I just got inspired," Lucas said. He stood up and kissed

the top of Hope's head. "You inspire me. Wait here." Lucas dashed away, out the door of Paddy's.

Hope didn't know what to think. She played with the ice cubes in her glass, drummed her fingers on the table. The waiter brought over a basket of crackers. She ripped open a Saltine pack. Where had Lucas gone?

"Could I get a refill, too?" Hope demanded, holding out her flat Diet Coke with its squeezed lemon slice perched atop the melting ice.

Paddy's swarmed with people Hope had never seen before, but she liked it better this way. So far, her relationship with Lucas had been under wraps. Not even Lenora or Pam knew about Lucas. From the moment she'd met him, Hope had always intended on keeping Lucas secret, but her success at doing so had astounded even her. In a short time, she'd gotten good, really good, at playing the game.

Across the booth from Hope, Lucas's backpack lay against the side of the table. Hope stared at the zipper on the pocket, half-undone. She could make out a few of the items from the inside poking out. One of the items looked like the notebook Lucas was always carrying with him. He wrote in it whenever he got the chance. Songs, mostly — or at least that was what Lucas told her.

The waiter brought the Coke refill, and Hope sat up to readjust her crinkled skirt. At the same time, she leaned across and fingered the top of the backpack. Should she?

Hope grabbed for the pack. With one easy tug, she removed the notebook and placed it carefully on the seat next to her. The cover was plain, with a mottled black-and-white pattern. A NO WAY OUT sticker had been plastered over the Name/Address block on the front. Additional pieces of paper stuck out at the top and on the side. Lucas had wrapped elastic around the spine to hold it together. She settled back into the booth and opened the cover.

Return to Lucas Wheeler if found.

Hope looked up at the front door of Paddy's. No one.

The inside front cover listed Lucas's address, but not his address in Chesterfield. This was a Massachusetts address. The notebook had been around for a long time.

Hope glanced over at Paddy's door again. Lucas was nowhere to be seen. She had no idea how long it would take him to come back. What if he appeared and saw her holding the notebook?

With one kick, Hope knocked the backpack, zipper still unzipped, to the floor. This way, she figured, when Lucas showed up she could quickly toss the notebook onto the floor, pretending that the pack had just fallen and all the contents had spilled out.

That would work.

Hope turned back to the notebook. She flipped through the first few pages. Key words caught her eyes as she skimmed for something, anything.

Just friends . . .
by the river . . .
don't ask . . .

Enrique says no way . . .
can't pass the test . . .
missing her . . .
Mom would never . . .
took some pills . . .
can't go on . . .

The pages were like candy. She couldn't stop reading.

Everyone has the answers here. But they're gone. My friends don't get me plain and simple. Even Rebecca tells me that she gets me but she's faking ALL the time. We live in a world of fakers but I need the truth. I need something. I need Dad to stop his drinking, stop leaving me. I need to let go, get out. I need to stop. I need Mom back. She was the only one who understood my music, the only one.

Hope's eyes shot to the door. The little bells over the door would give warning when Lucas came back.

"Miss?"

Hope nearly leaped out of her skin. She looked up at the waiter.

"Can I get you something else?" the waiter asked.

"No, we're still waiting for our food. We ordered like fifteen minutes ago," Hope said, waving him off as if he was a fly.

"Oh yes," the waiter replied, checking his order book. "I'm so sorry. Let me check on that for you."

"Moron," Hope muttered under her breath. She

glanced around. No one looked beyond their meatloaf blue plate specials.

Jingle jangle.

Door check. Hope glanced up. Someone was coming but it wasn't Lucas. An overweight family of six pushed inside the diner.

Hope looked back down at the notebook, flipping more pages. What was Lucas talking about?

My broken arm and ankle are starting to heal. At last. The doctor says it's a miracle that I survived the crash.

Hope skipped back to the pages from a few days before. She could feel her pulse pound—even in her fingertips—as she turned pages, further back.

Still trapped. I'm an idiot. How did I end up here? Where am I supposed to go now? I can still hear the crash inside my head, glass breaking, the sound of bones. That moment when I woke up in the hospital and Dad told me everything. That moment when I knew she was gone. If only I'd said when I saw the other car coming. But I didn't say a fucking thing. Why did it have to happen like this? I want her back. I want to rewind the clock, take it all back. The doctor says it will take a month or more for my cuts to heal. It's like this constant pain I can never lose. God, I am so lost. Will I always feel like this?

The door bells jangled again. With a knee-jerk reaction, Hope dropped the notebook and fell to the floor. But this time, there was no need to check the door.

She knew it was Lucas. Her heart was pumping like an engine.

"What are you doing down there?" Lucas asked.

"Oh, wow, Lucas," Hope said, trying not to sound so anxious. She efficiently stuffed the notebook and some of the other contents back into the pack, struggling with the zipper.

"I'm such a klutz," Hope said. "I kicked my foot up and knocked over your bag. I guess you left the zipper open. Everything went all over the place. . . ."

"Don't worry," Lucas said, helping Hope up. "I should have . . . what fell out?"

"Pencils," Hope lied. "A CD. A notebook. I just put everything back in but now it all won't fit. . . ."

"It's okay," Lucas said. When Hope was standing, he pulled one arm out from behind his back. "Aren't you going to ask about your surprise?" he said, grinning. Then he presented Hope with a single flower, an orange lily with petals as wide as wings.

"They didn't have roses," Lucas added regretfully as Hope accepted the flower. "I ran to Parkway Florist, but they had a lousy selection. I couldn't come back empty-handed so I grabbed this."

Briefly, Hope wished that Lucas *had* jogged even farther away to another florist on the other side of town to get a rose. Not because she'd much rather have that flower, but because it would have bought her more time to read from Lucas's journal.

She had only just gotten to the good parts: the parts about the accident.

No sooner did Lucas and Hope sit back down again than the food arrived. Hope let Lucas do most of the talking, for a change. Her eyes pinched into a squint as she tried to see through all of his talk. She'd told Lucas that their whole relationship was based on secrets, but the secrets inside his journal had topped the list. He was better at this than she'd given him credit for. What else didn't she know?

"You're not eating," Lucas said, nodding at Hope's salad plate. "Not like that's a big surprise or anything, but I'm starved. Do you mind?"

Lucas grinned and twirled pasta around his fork before taking a saucy mouthful. Hope watched him suck a strand of spaghetti. She reached across the table to wipe stray tomato sauce from his chin.

"Mmhank you," Lucas mumbled, still chewing.

The waiter reappeared. "Anything else I can get you two?" he asked.

Hope was about to say, "No, thanks. Now, please get lost." But just then, Lucas looked up from his plate and abruptly slid off his seat, ducking down beneath the table quickly, like he'd been shot. He was still holding his fork.

"Lucas?" For an instant, Hope worried. "What are you doing?" she asked, ducking under the booth herself. "Are you trying to be funny, because it's not funny when you—"

"Shhhhh." Lucas stuck his hand over Hope's mouth.

Hope bumped her head. "Ouch," she whispered and then got very quiet again. What *was* underneath this booth table anyway? The floor was a little wet from everyone's slushy shoes. Hope had nightmare visions of pink gum stuck to her hair. "What are we doing down here?" she whispered, absently rubbing her scalp.

"Cady," Lucas said. "I just saw Cady Sanchez in the doorway."

"Cady?"

Hope's heart pumped a little harder. Maybe this was the best thing that could happen. Maybe.

"Why is Cady here?" Hope asked. "I thought we agreed that no one we know ever comes here. Ever."

"I don't know, I don't know." Lucas was clearly shaken up.

"Well, shouldn't we check and see if she's really there before we have a total freak-out?" Hope suggested, getting up slowly.

She peered over the divider between their table and the rest of the diner, past the giant fish tank and Paddy's cage, and over to the front door. No one was there, or at least no one Hope recognized, except for Lorenzo, the owner, who was tacking up some flyers on the bulletin board.

"I don't see Cady, Lucas," Hope said. "You can sit up now."

Lucas slid back into the upright position in the booth. He looked a little clammy from all the commotion. A spray of spaghetti sauce marked the front of his shirt.

"Well, *that* was awkward," Hope snarled. "You want to tell me what that was about?"

"I just thought . . . I saw . . . she was standing right over . . . I didn't want her to see you . . . us . . . ."

Hope frowned. "Whatever. She's gone now—if she was ever here."

"Sorry," Lucas said, going back for more to eat.

After another bite, he looked up, astonished, like he'd been seized by a memory.

"Oh my God, Hope, I know why Cady was here. I completely forgot that the other day she told me she was tutoring some kid in guitar on this side of town. How could I have forgotten that?"

"I wonder," Hope said sarcastically.

Hope wanted to cling to the Cady thing, and shoot a few more meaningful (and dirty) looks at Lucas, but she had to let it go. There would be time enough to find out more about Lucas's relationship with Cady. She poked a fork into the pile of lettuce on her plate and moved her food from one side of the plate to the other.

"You know what?" Hope said. "My friends and I have decided that we want to go to more of your Hornets soccer games."

"Actual games?" Lucas asked. "I thought you guys just hung out at practices."

"That's because the tanning is optimum on the soccer field," Hope said. "You know that."

"You're not kidding, are you?" Lucas said.

Hope shook her head and they laughed together. She picked up the orange lily from the table.

"You know, this really is a nice flower," Hope said. "Thank you for getting it."

"You're welcome," Lucas said.

He reached for her hand, the one without the flower in it. She squeezed back.

"I just wish I knew everything there was to know about you," Hope mused.

"You and my psychiatrist," Lucas said.

"You see a shrink?" Hope asked with a look of feigned surprise.

"I'm not crazy. The doctor helps me sort out things."

"Things?"

"Life, death," Lucas said. He paused. "People like you."

Although she knew he was kidding around, Hope prickled at the joke.

"So what does your shrink know that I don't know?" she asked. "What happened in Boston?"

"Happened?" Lucas pulled away and hung his head.

"What is it?" Hope asked. "Did I ask the wrong thing? Or the right thing?"

"I wish I could tell you." Lucas sighed. "But I made a promise to myself that I wouldn't talk about it, not all of it anyway, not for a long time, until everything felt just right."

"Oh," Hope said, pretending to be satisfied. "Fine."

She shot a look at the backpack.

What did it matter what Lucas admitted? Hope didn't need him to do the talking anymore. Later that very night when they'd left Paddy's and were down in his basement, Hope could check Lucas's notebook again, by herself.

And she could check it again the next time she was over at his house and he was out running. Hope could keep on checking until she'd read every last confession, until she knew the inside of Lucas Wheeler as well as she knew herself.

Chapter Four

January 17, 5:02 PM
Cady

Red and yellow strings of lights shimmered on the walls inside Wonderland Ice Rink. Someone had placed a blow-up palm tree on top of a giant speaker in honor of Hawaiian Hula week, a Chesterfield tradition that brought "a little bit of summer to a town in the dead of winter." At least that was how the rink advertised it.

Cady held back, fingers on the rink railing. She wasn't ready for this. Everywhere, kids hung together in packs of four and five. It was a typical scene for a January Chesterfield weekend. There weren't too many other places to go in town. A Dave Matthews Band song pumped through the sound system as skaters took to the ice on dull blades, wearing plastic colored leis around their necks in honor of the occasion—and free with admission throughout the week.

This was no rink for show-offs. It was sardine-packed with kids of all ages and their parents and grandparents. The ice turned into a rainbow of mittens and hats and gloves and parkas as skaters danced, whirled, and yes, fell. If one kid tripped on ice, a few more were destined to tumble, too, because for every action on an ice rink, there was an immediate reaction. It was like a four-car pileup on the expressway, only wetter and much, much colder.

Marisol made her way over to Cady with a cup of hot

chocolate. "Didn't you see me and Bebe? We're over there. I can't believe it, but that guy Ed is here from my literature class."

"The newly cute one?" Cady joked. Ed had been in school with them since third grade, but only recently had he changed his look from "Neanderthal Geek" to "Guy With Potential."

"Yes, yes, ha ha," Marisol said. "And he's skating solo."

Cady looked around the crowd. "I was sort of hoping I might see Lucas Wheeler here tonight," she said.

"Well, it's your lucky night. I *just* saw him with a couple of guys from chem class," Marisol said.

Cady's eyes lit up. "You did?"

The two of them walked around the periphery of the rink, right past a group of kids from the hockey team. As usual, those boys were showing off their speed-skating skills for the girls.

The swathe of kids across the ice made Cady's head whirl — and she hadn't even had anything to drink. Of course, alcohol wasn't allowed here, but certain kids would find ways to sneak stuff into Gatorade bottles or even plain bottled water. Most kids walked a tightrope on Saturday nights, staying at least half-sober. Otherwise the ice patrol (aka the security guards at the rink) would get suspicious.

"There's your dream boy," Marisol said, subtly pointing to two guys standing over by the video games. Lucas stood at the right, hands in the back pockets of his Levis. Cady could tell what kind of jeans he wore from all the way over here. Naturally, she'd been staring at him from behind for weeks, even before she'd officially met him at the New Year's party.

Bebe ran over to Marisol and Cady, wearing three Hawaiian leis.

"*Aloha,*" she said, placing leis on Cady and Marisol.

"*Aloha* yourself," Cady said.

"You look cute tonight," Bebe said to Cady.

"You think?" Cady asked. "I didn't know what to wear. What do you wear for ice hula? I mean, it's not like I've got a grass skirt in my closet—"

"I think maybe you need to take a breath," Marisol said, laughing.

"Either that or take some serious drugs," Bebe joked.

"Very funny," Cady said. "I just want to look good . . . you know? Special? Is there anything wrong with that? Because Lucas and I meet up once in a while at school but that's not like seeing him here where every other girl in our class probably has their sharpened hooks out—"

"Cady, would you slow down? What are you talking about?" Marisol said.

"I wish I'd brought my guitar."

"Yeah," Marisol said. "The guitar would be key. The guitar is where you and Lucas really connect. I'd go home and get the guitar."

"You think?" Cady asked. "Should I go home and get Fred?"

When she was younger, Cady had nicknamed her guitar Fred. She knew it was a funny name, like Bert or Ernie from *Sesame Street*, but she liked calling it that. Mom and Dad always said that Cady's guitar was like an imaginary friend who talked back — but with music instead of words. Fred was her one true steady companion, surviving all the junior high cliques, monster zits, pop math quizzes, and even unrequited crushes.

"No Fred, Cady," Marisol said, shaking her head and laughing as Bebe giggled. She threw her arm around her friend. "You can do this alone. Trust me."

"Does my hair look good pulled back or should I let it down?" Cady asked, still acting fidgety.

"Cady, come on. You look way better than the usual generic girls," Bebe said.

"Yeah," Marisol added. "Take Lenora Less or Hope White, for example . . ."

Marisol indicated the group of girls standing in a huddle on the ice nearby. The matched set of four "it" girls wore color-coordinated parkas. For as far back as Cady could remember, Hope was classified as the prettiest girl in school. She may as well have worn a sign around her neck that said CHESTERFIELD ROYALTY. She'd been voted freshman class queen, sophomore class queen, and junior class queen. This year she'd probably be voted senior class queen. Cady resented Hope for always getting what she wanted.

"Hope's a baaaad example, Marisol," Cady said, making a goat sound. "Put me and Hope in a room and who would Lucas Wheeler pick?"

"You," Marisol and Bebe said at exactly the same time.

"Come on . . ." Cady said. "That's what my best friends

are supposed to say, but it doesn't mean it's even close to the truth."

"Marisol's right," Bebe said. "Lucas would absolutely choose you, Cady. Anyway, haven't you and Hope already been in a room together when he picked you? Like New Year's Eve?"

"Yeah," Marisol said. "Lucas spent the whole night talking to Y-O-U and not Miss Perfect, right? Right? And what did you talk about?"

"Guitars," Cady said with a smile.

"See? Guitars are the key! I told you," Marisol said.

"Not to mention the fact that you look hyper hot in that sweater," Bebe said. She made a sizzle sound like frying bacon. "Your boobs even look bigger than usual."

"I wish!" Cady said, glancing down at her chest. "It's just my period. God, do I look puffy all over?"

"Hmmm. Let's not share *those* thoughts with Lucas, shall we?" Marisol teased.

"Yes, I would save that for the next meeting of the Way Too Much Information Club," Bebe joked.

Cady laughed. "Okay, okay, you guys win."

"Face it. You look good," Marisol said again, reassuring her.

"Damn good," Bebe said with emphasis.

"Okay, I'm going for it."

Cady gave her friends a wide smile, but hesitated another moment before moving toward Lucas and the other boys. She didn't want it to seem too obvious where she was going. But it was hard to look unobtrusive while wobbling around on skate guards.

Bebe and Marisol chased after her.

"Cady," they called, "just skate across the middle of the ice. He's right there."

Cady worried about crossing the crowded ice. But her friends convinced her to take the fastest route. So once Marisol had removed Cady's skate guards, and with a gentle shove from Bebe, Cady started her short journey, clumsily maneuvering her way around the hockey players and the show-offs. She nearly lost her balance twice, which made her wish that she hadn't given up on skating lessons so many years before.

As Cady inched along the ice quasi-successfully, she practiced lines in her head, thinking about what she would say that might sound friendly, romantic, or suggestive — or all three. Or maybe she'd just stick to guitar talk for a while.

As Cady approached the dead center of the rink, she managed to avoid skaters left and right. Remembering Bebe's comment on the sweater, Cady threw back her shoulders hoping it made her chest stick out.

The next thing she knew, she was flat on her back on the ice, and a little girl, maybe eight years old, was standing over her, wailing.

"What's your problem?" a woman called out from the sidelines. Shaking a fist in the air, the woman slid over toward the scene of the collision on her shoes (no skates). "You older kids think you own the ice, don't you? I saw what happened. You're not supposed to cross in the middle. Don't you know anything?" the woman screamed at Cady.

Cady could feel a bump blooming at the back of her head. The little girl's mother was raging like a lunatic.

"I'm going to have you thrown off the ice," the mother threatened as she helped her daughter up. The little girl wore leggings with sequins down the side and sky-blue eye shadow. Her life story played inside Cady's head like a bad movie: ice skating lessons from dusk till dawn; pushy mother; nail tips at ten; frostbite. She knew the type.

Cady blinked so she wouldn't see double. Wasn't anyone coming to check on her and her massive head injury? She imagined her friends on the sidelines, laughing at her fall instead of coming over to help. Everyone from school had probably seen the crash, including Hope White.

Where was Lucas?

Cady pushed herself up from the cold, wet slush on the surface of the rink. Her skates clicked as she tried getting to her feet. The mother of the girl was still screaming, and she didn't offer to help Cady up. One of the ice rink staff had come by to escort the mother and her little ice princess off the ice. The staff member gave Cady a not-so-stern warning, but nothing more. Even he didn't help her up.

"Nice fall, Sanchez," Cady heard someone say. She looked up, her hair in a wet tangle. A guy named Wesley from her chemistry class was standing there. Next to him was Lucas. They must have seen her fall.

"How is it down there?" Wesley asked.

"A little cold," Cady said plainly, trying really hard to keep her teeth from chattering.

"Skate much?" Lucas asked, grinning. He extended his hands.

Cady grabbed on and pulled herself up to her feet, wobbling a little.

"Man, that kid did a triple salchow and you went down, Cady," Lucas joked. "Everyone saw it. Wish I had a videocam."

"Everyone saw? Just great," Cady mumbled.

"No one really saw," Lucas said. "I was only kidding." He touched her shoulder.

Cady took a deep breath. "Oh."

A few feet away, in the blur of people at the edge of the rink, Cady spotted Marisol and Bebe, her own personal cheering section. Their arms waved and spun madly like two whirligigs, and Cady could only imagine what *they* were saying about her smooth landing.

Cady glanced up — way up — at the rafters of the ice rink. A couple of trapped Mylar balloons had their strings caught in the beams overhead like seaweed. A voice came over the loudspeaker, but no one could translate what the woman said. Then the music came up again, louder than before. Wesley skated away to get something to drink.

"They didn't have ice luaus like this back at my old school in Massachusetts," Lucas commented.

"Chesterfield's one of a kind," Cady said.

"I know you're probably a little shell-shocked by what happened," Lucas said as Cady finally shook off all the ice dust that had covered her pants. "And I'm sorry to laugh. But it *was* a little funny the way that girl's mother came out here screaming her head off. You would laugh if it were me standing in your shoes — er, skates."

Lucas put on a mock announcer voice.

" 'Of course, if your butt freezes, Ms. Cady, the rink won't be held accountable. . . . ' "

With that comment, Cady did laugh — right out loud.

Lucas laughed, too. He threw his head back, and Cady saw a little scar under his chin.

"What's that?" she asked, reaching over to touch it.

Lucas felt for the scar. "This?" he said, getting a little serious again. "Slipped on a pool ladder. Came down hard."

"Ouch."

"Yeah, it was an all-points bulletin. They had to drain the entire city pool, I heard," Lucas said. "Water turned pink, there was so much blood. Some cuts are like that, you know? I am like the most accident-prone person I know."

"I think I may have you beat on that one," Cady said, pointing to the welt on her head.

The announcer read off the titles of a few songs and then invited everyone onto the ice for Ladies' Choice.

"How about a quick spin?" Lucas asked.

Cady shook her head. "You go ahead. I'm sure some other lady will choose you."

A group of girls dashed by, skates whizzing. Pam, Lenora, and Hope were out in front of the pack. They nearly collided with Lucas.

But Lucas didn't say a word to them. He turned back to Cady and extended his elbow. Cady grabbed onto it like a life preserver.

"So what were you doing out there?" Lucas asked.

"Coming to see you, actually," Cady admitted, feeling bold.

"Me?"

"Yeah, well . . ."

"I'm glad," Lucas said. Cady could tell he was flirting.

They skated over to one of the ice rink off-ramps. As soon as Cady was seated, Lucas bent down and unlaced her skates. She sat there as he pulled off each skate and rubbed her feet.

"Thanks," Cady said awkwardly.

"Feeling better?" Lucas asked.

"Yeah."

Lucas reached into his pocket to warm his hands. He pulled out his spare change and fished through for one small penny.

"Next time you skate, bring this," he said. "It's really old and it's good luck. I swear. Worked for me so far."

"Thanks," Cady smiled. She took the tarnished penny, and pressed it into her own zippered pocket. "So you believe in luck?" she asked.

"And fate," Lucas said offhandedly.

"Oh," Cady said.

"We really do have to get together to play music soon," Lucas said.

"Yes," Cady said simply.

The loudspeaker interrupted with some message about a Hawaiian sunset.

Lucas pointed up.

High above their heads, a projected orange light spread across the ceiling and rafters. The crowd ooohed.

Cady thought about how sunsets — real or fake — always looked so beautiful.

And quietly, Cady wondered why she'd always understood endings so much better than anything else.

Chapter Three

January 9, 4:11 PM
Lucas

Lucas's tendons had been bugging him lately, and the weather had been ice-floe cold, but he kept up the regular runs. He tried to get out most mornings before breakfast and school, but occasionally he'd jog in the afternoon. Sometimes he turned on his iPod to tune out the world, while other times he just let the songs of birds and traffic fill his head.

His feet pounded on the hard, cold asphalt. His laces kept coming undone, and the soles were shot.

Westerly St.

Okay, Lucas told himself, as he zigzagged up the short hill, huffing. His toes were pressing into the front of the shoe. He didn't want to lose another toenail. One shoelace flapped on the ground, and he prayed that he wouldn't trip. Just a few more yards and he'd be at the crest. Then he could stop.

Krandall Rd.

Lucas slowed and surveyed the neighborhood from up here. He'd been around the manor area of Chesterfield many times before now, although it hadn't been on foot but inside his convertible. Lucas tried to remember which streets led back down to the main part of Chesterfield, which was where he eventually needed to go, and which led out to the parkways with routes to the Chesterfield beach. Although the town seemed small, he often found himself getting lost. But he kept running.

Lucas told his dad, Aunt Rita, and his new therapist, Dr. Shakely, that the move to this new town seemed to be working out. Naturally, Lucas had his problems, but he just didn't feel like overanalyzing his new life. Not yet.

He'd come so far since a little more than a year ago, when he was locked up in Mass General with doctors all around him.

After the accident with Mom, he'd been through a blender of therapists, each one asking questions and churning up all the stuff inside that ached.

The only therapy he truly wanted right now was music.

He'd been surprised (*so* surprised) to meet that dark-haired girl on New Year's Eve. What was her name again? Katie? Kitty? No. Cady was her name. How could he have forgotten that beautiful name?

Cady was short for Cadence.

"It means rhythm or flow of sounds," Cady had told him at the party.

It wasn't the girl but her guitar that drew Lucas in at first. But Cady's smile kept him interested. Cady's contagious, toothy smile was framed by naturally full lips that only seemed to get fuller the more she talked. It was hard to turn away from those lips. It was even harder to resist the urge to kiss them.

Cady was a little like Lucas with the music and the guitar. She was even a little like his ex-girlfriend, Rebecca, as much as he hated to admit it. Lucas didn't want to think he had a type, but Cady and Rebecca had the same curly brown hair and fair skin. The person Cady reminded Lucas of the most, however, was his own mom. Jesus, his therapists would have a field day with that one.

Sometimes Lucas could remember so few things about his mother, and then all of a sudden he would meet a person who had Mom's nose or brown eyes, or even her cinnamon scent.

Meadow Ln.

Lucas caught his breath. He started to walk a little instead of run, shaking out his feet. His legs felt heavy. He'd had too many beers, Tostitos, and Devil Dogs over the holidays in a lame attempt to drown his anxieties. If Lucas had any hopes of making the spring soccer team at Chesterfield, he needed to drop a few pounds and firm up his pecs.

Lucas crossed his ankles one over the other and leaned over to touch his toes. The blood rushed down to his scalp, and he hung down there, breathing deeply. He saw double when he lifted his head up too fast.

Lucas wasn't looking for a girlfriend, was he? Cady had a friend, he remembered, named Marisol, who had a zesty personality. He'd noticed a pretty Asian girl at the party, too. She was in his history class and seemed really smart. Maybe she was available? Of course, Lucas thought about that blond girl, Hope, too. He'd never met someone who talked to him — or *at* him — the way Hope did. She came into that kitchen at the party all dressed up with pink ribbons on the hem and cuffs of her low-cut shirt, but there were all these sharp edges underneath, poking out like thorns, and he liked it. He wasn't sure why, but Lucas liked it.

Lucas stretched up and rubbed his shoulder. The run back home from here would be difficult. Had he gone too far? Slowly, he accelerated back into the road, at more of a trot now than a run, and headed down a steep hill toward the main part of Chesterfield. Or at least that was where he hoped he was headed. He tried to keep an eye out for black ice.

The street dead-ended into a peeling, yellow steel barrier that cut the road off from a small running stream. Lucas paused to look over the edge, but he saw no fish, only litter caught in the brambles and a few black geese poking their bills into the iced-over muck. For some reason, the geese in Chesterfield had stopped flying south for the winter. Lucas always bitched that it was all the global warming.

He jogged around a curve into the town proper, past the police station. He slowed down to look at a woman, bundled up, pacing on the grass in Davidson Park, a wide stretch of grass in the middle of town. She had a couple of Labrador retriever pups on leashes. They could barely walk on their new paws.

Lucas looked up at the trees, down at the path, and over, far over, at a lineup of city buildings. Up a little farther on one park path, he saw something, or rather someone, familiar. A blond girl was tossing a bag into one of the iron garbage cans nearby. She had on patent leather boots. Who could walk in those shoes?

Hope.

Lucas stumbled, but then quickly jogged toward her.

"Hope?" Lucas called out.

Hope turned and looked at Lucas with a blank expression. Then Lucas said his own name, and a glimmer of recognition spread across her face.

"Oh, Lucas. *Duh*, of course," Hope said, smiling sweetly. "What are you doing here? You're not stalking me or anything, are you?" she joked, her eyes sparkling.

"No, I was out running," Lucas started to say. "I can't believe this. I was just . . . well, I was running along and . . . I just can't believe you're right here. This is tripping me out."

"Me too." Hope grinned. "Glad to see you," she said.

Lucas wanted to confess to Hope that he had been thinking about her that very moment when she'd appeared, like a phantom, in the middle of the sidewalk. But he worried that might scare her off.

On the gold bracelet she wore, Lucas saw Eiffel Tower and pyramid charms and a large, painted enamel letter *H* for Hope.

"I work over there," Hope said, pointing to the office buildings in the distance. "Gateway Medical. Just answering phones and filing. My dad makes me work so I'm not always bugging him for money. You know the drill."

"Oh," Lucas said, still dumbstruck. "Sure. Yeah. Of course."

"So, you're a runner, huh?" Hope asked. Lucas could tell she was checking out his thighs and the rest of his physique.

"I run," Lucas said. "I'd like to say I'm athletic, but these days I'm a little off my game."

"What are you talking about?" Hope said. "You have a great body, even if you're covered up with sweats."

Lucas was glad that he wasn't the kind of guy who blushed easily, because he would have turned magenta at that remark. It wasn't just what Hope said, he noticed. It was *how* she said it, with her hip jutting out to one side, arms crossed in front of her just under her chest. It wasn't that she looked at him, it was *how* she looked at him.

And she had a good body, too. Lucas had thought so before, at the party, but everything had happened so fast then that he didn't have a chance to take it all in. Now, standing there on the park path in the middle of winter, he had that chance.

Hope's hairline looked slightly darker than the rest of her hair, and so Lucas guessed maybe she dyed it to get that shade of model blond. She had long, piano-player fingers, too.

"Are you a musician?" Lucas asked, before he could stop himself.

"Me?" Hope laughed. "Um . . . no. I can't even play a tambourine."

"That's okay," Lucas said, a little disappointed. "You ever try guitar or piano? Because you have these awesome fingers . . ."

"Awesome, huh?" Hope dangled them out in front of him. "Why thank you."

Lucas held the bottom of his chin thoughtfully. It was his Rodin pose. In the past, girls always liked it when it seemed as if he was taking them in, calculating, counting, and cataloging all of their assets.

"You have nice ears," Lucas blurted.

"Ears? Well, that's a new one."

222

"No, I mean . . . under your hat. I like to notice the things that no one else does," Lucas said.

"I noticed you right away," Hope said quickly, stepping a little closer.

Lucas shuffled from foot to foot. "Yeah," he said, masking his discomfort. It was just like the night in the kitchen, only this was in slow motion, close but not quite touching.

"We should get together sometime," Hope suggested, looking up at Lucas.

Lucas glanced away. "Gee, I don't know . . ." he muttered, trying hard not to break into laughter. He did that sometimes when he was nervous.

Hope took a baby step back and reached into the zippered orange leather clutch that she had under her arm. She pulled out a fat black marker and bit off the cap.

"Here," she said, grabbing Lucas's hand.

She opened his fingers and wrote on his palm.

"Here's my number."

Lucas held up his hand and repeated the numbers.

"Why don't you give me a call?" Hope asked.

"Okay," Lucas said. What else could he say? Then he remembered the other guy from the kitchen. "Uh . . . what about your boyfriend?"

"Ancient, ancient history," Hope said.

Lucas smiled at her remark, although he knew it couldn't possibly be true. A guy she'd been locking lips with a week before was *not* ancient history. Not even close.

"I can't believe I ran into you like this," Lucas said.

"Who says there are no meaningful coincidences?" Hope asked, playing with the hem of her fancy coat. She had it lifted up so Lucas could see above her knees. She wore a skirt and no stockings, even though it was cold.

"Maybe I'll see you around school," Lucas said.

Hope shrugged. "Maybe not," she teased. "Maybe I'll just see you around in my dreams."

Without another word Hope walked on down the path.

Lucas felt a ripple go through his body. It was the same sensation he always got at the amusement park when he was backed up against the spinning ride where the floor fell out.

"See you," he called out after Hope. She was sashaying from side to side like a dancer, arms swinging freely in the air. She knew he was staring, didn't she? Lucas kept waiting for her to turn around once more, but she didn't. He watched as Hope crossed another path and made a beeline for an office building with a gigantic number three sculpture out in front.

Lucas looked down at his inked palm and repeated the numbers there inside his head. Maybe, he thought to himself, he'd play those numbers at BLOTTO and see what came up. He'd always been a lousy gambler, but something here — a spark — had been ignited. Her name fit, too: *Hope*.

After leaving Davidson Park, Lucas jogged across the street in the direction of a small takeout Chinese place, the kind with the disgusting close-up photos of General Tso chicken and chow mein in the window. Then he made a left at the corner and turned into the lobby of another stone office building.

Brass name plaques hung on the wall where he walked in. From there, the entryway led to several office doors shut tight. There was no reception area, just orange and brown chairs parked in front of each of the rooms, and a few ragged copies of *Time* and *Sports Illustrated.*

Lucas plopped down onto a brown chair and checked his watch. For once, he was early. He leaned forward, then back, kicking the toe of his sneaker along the shag rug. A chunk of ice came off. He glanced up. A few ceiling tiles appeared to be stained with water damage. Sweat dripped down his back from the run. He wished he had a towel and a new sweatshirt.

After about five minutes, a woman came out of one of the offices with a pen and notepad in her hands.

"Mr. Wheeler? Lucas Wheeler?"

Lucas stood up and wiped his hands on his sweats.

"Hey, Doc," Lucas said, tentatively shaking her hand. "Sorry, about the . . . I was out running before I got here and I didn't think I'd be so . . ."

"No problem, Mr. Wheeler. Come right in," the doctor said. "I've been waiting for you."

Hurriedly, Lucas followed Dr. Shakely into a beige office, where he took a seat in a beige chair.

It was time to begin again.

Chapter Two

December 31, 11:31 PM
Hope

Emile's New Year's Eve party was packed with kids. They flowed from the front porch into the hall and living room and back into the kitchen. Some kids drifted onto the patios, even though the thermometer read an icy 31 degrees. An Outkast tune had been cranked up to volume ten, and everyone wanted to dance, but the living room felt a little too much like a mosh pit.

The size of the crowd was unexpected. Emile prided himself on being the class party king. He had a kickoff bash every September, a New Year's blowout on December 31st, and a rave at the end of school. Attendance was up from last year's New Year's Eve. This year, Emile had extended personal invites to everyone at the high school. He liked to think he was everyone's friend. And maybe he was, if such a thing was possible.

Inside Emile's house, Hope stood near a tall ficus tree planted in a terra-cotta pot in the corner of the living room. She carefully watched as a kid she'd never really paid much attention to before now, Lucas Wheeler, entered Emile's kitchen through its swinging door.

Lucas had a swagger that Hope picked up on. She liked the way he moved around the room. Since Lucas had arrived at Emile's party, Hope watched him move from classmate to classmate, plastic cup in hand. He'd gone over to the long wooden table that served as the bar and poured something brown — probably Scotch. Or maybe it was just beer? After circling the couch, Lucas had finally cozied up on the sofa next to Cady Sanchez and her guitar.

He sat too close, Hope thought as she watched Lucas rest his hand on Cady's knee a few times. As soon as he did that, his swagger turned soft. And when Lucas grabbed Cady's guitar and then cradled it in his own lap like a baby? Cady probably loved that but Hope didn't like it one bit.

What was Cady Sanchez doing here anyway? Since when did Emile Duggan invite *her*? Hope hated to think that she was just some name on a list of party guests with the likes of Cady Sanchez and her lame friends Marisol Duran and Bebe Lynch. Hope liked to think she rated higher than that.

Hope looked over at Emile, standing by the bar, helping kids fill their cups with punch. Emile winked back. Hope smiled.

Sure, Hope knew the truth about his party invitations. Emile wanted to get into every girl's pants, and many complied, no questions asked. He had been trying (and failing) to get it on with Hope since tenth grade, so she knew the deal as well as anyone.

Hope never told Emile no, not exactly. She never told any guy flat out "NO." She liked the game of chase way too much. For as long as Hope could remember, guys wanted to be with her, and they would do anything to let her know that. It was fun to play along. It was fun to step over the line and then jump back.

But Lucas, he was different.

Everything about Lucas screamed "come and get me." After all, he was the only new senior, which usually meant something important when a kid transferred into Chesterfield late in the high school years. Hope figured that in this particular case, it meant Lucas was deep trouble. That smelled delicious.

And standing there, watching him with the guitar, with Cady's knee, Hope could tell a lot about Lucas. It was the way he used his hands. He liked to touch things. Maybe he liked it *too* much?

Hope's mind reeled. The Cady Sanchez factor only intensified Hope's desire to keep Lucas for herself. There was no way Hope could let Cady get something—*someone*—this ripe.

Cady never seemed to worry about the way she looked or the way she acted. Shouldn't there be a price to pay for that kind of confidence? Hope worried all the time about how she looked and who she knew. She had to. It mattered.

Cady wrote poems and sang out loud, right out loud in front of huge crowds at the local coffeehouse, and never flinched, not once. Cady had perfect brown, curly hair and this exotic, faraway look that invited stares. Hope knew the only way she got stares was by pushing it—all of it—right out there into the world. Cady was the kind of girl who would never really get lost, because her heart was just too damn big.

Back in elementary school, Hope and Cady had spent hours and days and weeks playing dolls and trucks and making up students in their own imaginary school. They called themselves the Borrowers, after the little characters in the famous books, because they liked to borrow each other's clothes, homework, and everything else. Hope was light, Cady was dark. They balanced each other.

Until junior high, when everything got out of balance. That was when most girls got boobs but only some girls got boys. Hope and Cady branched off into different cliques, and then nothing between the two of them ever clicked again.

Here it was, their last year at Chesterfield, and Hope wanted back all those little shreds and scraps of herself that she felt she'd sacrificed for Cady or given away to Cady so long ago. But she'd have to take them. She'd have to *steal* them back.

And so right there, right next to the ficus tree, Hope got her brilliant idea. She came up with the most perfect game of chase that she would ever play. Cady wanted Lucas, but Hope would get him first. And if Hope couldn't have Lucas for herself, she'd make him suffer for it. She'd ruin him for everyone. She'd ruin everything with a lip-gloss smile.

Hope cocked her hip, licked her lips, and headed for the kitchen.

Swish-swoosh.

Hope wriggled through the door to Emile's kitchen with a grin on her face. Lucas stood there at the counter, hands on two cups filled with punch.

She barreled into him, knocking one of his cups into the sink.

"Happy New Year!" Hope said, giggling. She ran her

229

hands over the front of Lucas's shirt. "I didn't get you all wet, did I? I didn't realize that I would come through the doors like that. Silly me."

Lucas shrugged and shook out his hand. The spilled cup had gotten him a little wet on his wrist.

"No problem," Lucas mumbled.

"Great party, right?" Hope asked.

"Yes, I'm having a good time."

"You're the new kid, aren't you?" Hope asked. "What's your name again?"

"Lucas," he said. "And I've been around a few months. Do I know you?"

"Not exactly," Hope said, poking his chest with her index finger. "We can change that."

"I'm really bad with faces and names. Can you tell me —"

"Hope White."

Hope quickly dashed back over to the swinging door. This was the best way to start the game. She would pretend to leave but then pull herself right back into the room.

"Oops!" Hope said, backtracking. She tugged on her top, knowing that the harder she pulled, the more cleavage she could reveal. Then she danced back over to where Lucas stood.

"Forget something?" Lucas asked. She saw him look down her shirt.

Perfect.

"My drink," Hope said. "I forgot my drink. That was why I came in here in the first place, wasn't it?"

Hope hoisted herself up onto the countertop and took a

seat, crossing her legs as Lucas watched her. She knew her skirt was hiked just a little too high.

All at once the doors swung open and a couple of girls came in looking for beers for themselves and their boyfriends. As they walked out, beers in hand, Emile, the host, appeared.

"Hey!" Emile cried. "Hope, I was looking for you. We're almost ready to do the countdown."

"I was looking for you, too," Hope said, pretending to be nice, when really all she wanted to do was jump off the counter and Karate-chop her way over to the other side of the kitchen to kick Emile's ass.

Lucas looked confused. Hope realized in an instant that Emile's presence could actually *help* her plan, not hurt it. She threw herself at Emile and nuzzled his neck. Emile responded immediately by clutching Hope's backside with a firm squeeze. He was drunk, very drunk.

"Have you met Lucas?" Hope asked Emile, drawing back.

"Yeah," Emile said, still clutching. "I invited him, remember?"

"You two an item?" Lucas asked.

Hope leaned in and gave Emile a quick peck. She grabbed a beer off the counter and shoved it into his hand.

"Be a gentleman, Emile?" Hope said. "I promised I'd get a beer for Lenora. Could you bring this over to her for me?"

"Lenora's here?" Emile asked. "But I didn't see —"

"Go on," Hope said, practically tossing him out of the kitchen.

Hope turned around to face Lucas once Emile had left the room.

"He's a nice guy," Hope said. "But I just don't think that we're going to work out."

"But he's your boyfriend?" Lucas asked.

"Maybe not . . ."

"Oh."

As Lucas filled up his cup with punch, Hope grabbed his bicep.

"You work out?" she asked.

"Are you hitting on me?" Lucas asked. "Because your boyfriend is probably right outside that door."

"So?" Hope giggled. She stroked his arm some more.

"Been at Chesterfield a while?" Lucas asked. She could tell his breath was getting shallow. His eyes were on her chest.

"I've been here my whole life. Can you believe it?" She frowned.

Lucas nodded. "I just moved from Massachusetts last fall. I lived in Boston for most of my life."

"Why did you move?"

"You know. A bunch of reasons."

"What's the big mystery? You can tell me," Hope said.

She kept her hands on Lucas's arm and felt the muscle. He was bigger than she'd thought at first. She wondered if that was true about the rest of him, too. She and her girl-friend Lenora had a running tally of the boys in their class, arranged by size. Together, the two of them had made out with at least fourteen of the boys. They collected informa-tion about the other guys from other girls in class.

Lucas wasn't answering her question, so Hope leaned

over and stuck her fingers into the nearby ice bucket. She popped a cube into her mouth and then pulled it out and rubbed it along her slender neck.

"Whooooooo," Hope squealed.

Lucas smiled and stepped back. "Whoa. That was some scream."

"Sorry," Hope said.

"Nah, believe it or not, I collect sounds like that."

"Huh?"

"I collect sounds. Weird, right?"

"Right," Hope said. She didn't know where this conversation was going.

"I use sounds when I write my music. They inspire riffs. I mix them into my own tracks."

Hope *had* to change the subject. She couldn't talk about music.

"You're really cute," Hope blurted. She reached out to touch Lucas's face, but he moved her hand away.

"What are you doing?" Lucas asked. "I don't even know you."

"Isn't that the point? This is a party. You're supposed to have fun. Try new things. New people . . ."

Lucas laughed. "You're funny."

"Pour me a drink," Hope said, tossing her hair. "Will you? Lots of ice, though."

Lucas obeyed. She liked that. He poured the ice into the cup he'd been holding and then filled that with punch.

Hope took a sip. "So what are your New Year's resolutions?"

Lucas shrugged. "Have fun. Do good. You know."

"Do good?" Hope laughed. "I don't think so."

Lucas laughed right along with her. "You know, I'm a little drunk. I think it's impairing my judgment."

"Nothing about you is impaired, Lucas," Hope said.

The kitchen doors flew open again, and Hope leaned back, away from Lucas. She turned to the counter and poured her punch down the sink.

Lucas's buddy Wes burst into the small room clutching a few empties.

"Luke!" Wes said, strolling over. "You're blowing it out there."

Lucas ran his fingers through his hair. Hope pretended not to notice.

"I mean it, man. Some other dude just got your girl."

Lucas's eyes bugged out. "What are you talking about?" he asked, clearly trying to play it cool.

"Come on, man, you have work to do. Get your ass out there."

"Yeah, yeah," Lucas said, handing off another chilled Samuel Adams. "Here's one more for you and I'm coming out now."

Wes took the beer and shuffled out in a little bit of a stupor. Lucas turned back to Hope.

"Sorry," he said.

Hope stood on her toes and linked her fingers behind her neck so she was hanging on, literally. That got Lucas to bend closer.

Just as the clock turned to midnight she heard everyone in the living room let out a loud cheer.

"Happy New Year!" they screamed.

Then Hope planted a slow, wet kiss on Lucas's lips. She felt his body stiffen next to her. She could tell right away how much he wanted. The plan was working.

Hope pulled back just as quickly as she'd pulled forward. "Happy New Year," she said.

Lucas didn't move or speak.

It was exactly the reaction Hope wanted. Without a word, she bumped the swinging door with one hip and left the kitchen right where she'd found it.

As Hope walked into the next room she could still see Cady, sitting there — alone — on the sofa. Wes stood nearby, sucking down his beer.

Hope went back to her ficus tree and waited to see what would happen next.

It didn't take more than thirty seconds for Lucas to exit the kitchen carrying his punch cups. He made his way back to the sofa where Cady sat. Cady smiled as he handed her the drink. Hope saw Lucas curl one leg under and settle back. Then she saw him wipe his mouth with the back of his hand.

Hope popped her lips again. She heard some kids in a corner singing a familiar tune.

"Should auld acquaintance be forgot . . ."

Hope smiled. She hadn't forgotten one single thing.

This would most definitely be a New Year to remember.

Chapter One

December 31, 11:05 PM
Cady

"I'll be right back, I swear," Marisol said to Cady as they stood in Emile's living room. "Mama just called and I forgot to give her back the key to the other car. I promise I'll come right back and then we can look for that guy."

"You're just going to leave me here, by myself?" Cady asked, leaning on her guitar case.

"What are you talking about? Half of our grade is here. You know everyone in this room. You've known most people here since we were in first grade. And Bebe is coming soon." Marisol gave her a kiss on the cheek and started off.

"Marisol . . ."

"Cady, cheer up. It's New Year's Eve. Why don't you play a song for everyone?"

"Oh, now *that's* a good way to blend," Cady muttered, smirking.

Cady hated parties. She especially hated drinking parties. No one ever really acted the way they did in school. And the music usually sucked. On top of everything else, Cady was stressing out—a lot—about the coming year. About college and ending high school and all that. And there was the guy, too, the one she'd seen down by the music room a few times. He'd only started school that year, and Cady figured that he must play an instrument or sing or something.

But they'd never spoken. The only thing she really knew about him was his name: Lucas Wheeler.

As Marisol rushed away, Cady noticed a bowl of Cheetos on a long coffee table in front of a leather couch. Snacking would take the edge off. She motored for a seat, parked her guitar next to the arm of the couch, and plunged her hand into the bowl.

She was happy for Emile. He wasn't a good friend of hers but he seemed like a nice guy. And he'd worked really hard to get as many kids as possible to come to this year's New Year's party. He was always working the room to get people in a party mood. Tonight he was passing around shots of Jägermeister.

Cady didn't see the point in getting wasted. Somewhere along the way, maybe in junior year, she'd decided that she liked lucid better. She enjoyed the feeling of clarity, when she could sit down and write a good song. Anything else felt like cheating.

When she looked down, Cady realized that her fingertips were beginning to turn neon orange. She had to stop eating.

Kids pushed away from the couch, dancing to the thumping music. Standard hip-hop. Emile had one of those players with a hundred rotating CDs, and he'd tried to include as many different kinds of music as possible. The best Emile parties were raves, where he got some friends together to DJ. Unfortunately, no one could spin tonight.

Cady reached into her cowhide bag and took out a small notebook with a pen clipped to the side. If she had to sit here and wait for Marisol to come back, she'd at least work on one of her new songs. She flipped to a page with a few scribbles at the top.

I take the gloomy stage
To find a center for myself

"Is this seat taken?"

Cady whipped her head around to see a tall, lanky guy standing at the corner of the couch.

Him.

"Sorry," Lucas said. "I didn't mean to bug you."

"No!" Cady exclaimed, her face coloring. "What are you talking about? I was just spacing out. I always do that. Do you want to sit down?"

Cady shoved her notebook back into her bag and moved to the side. Then she invited Lucas to sit with an extended hand. Lucas accepted. He gently pushed his way around her guitar and moved right into the corner of the sofa.

"So, you're Cady, right?" Lucas asked. "I'm bad with names."

"Cadence, actually, Cady for short."

"Cadence?"

"It means rhythm or flow of sounds. Blame my dad. He's way into music and he's way too sentimental."

"I like it a lot," Lucas said.

"How's your senior year?" Cady asked. "I mean, you're new, right?"

"Chesterfield's okay," Lucas said, laughing. He reached for the bowl of Cheetos and stuffed some into his own mouth. Cady noticed that his fingers turned orange as he ate, too.

"Do you like the party so far?" Cady asked with real interest.

"So far . . ." Lucas said. "Considering I don't have too many friends here."

"I'll be your friend," Cady offered, meaning it.

Lucas grinned. He leaned back and took a breath.

"I moved here last summer, you know," Lucas explained. "From Massachusetts."

Slowly, he told Cady the rather complicated story of his journey from Boston to Chesterfield, about getting stuck in a rainstorm and getting a flat tire on the moving van and nearly colliding with a bus.

Lucas liked to talk. Cady liked to listen.

She took in his face, the square jaw that looked as if it actually may have been broken at one point. His dark eyes were so big; she'd never seen a boy with eyes so big and lashes so long. His teeth were crooked, too, and his nose was a little pink. He'd been drinking too much just like everyone else. She saw something on the inside of Lucas's wrist, too, a scar maybe, but she didn't say anything. Lucas used his hands a lot as he spoke.

"So, are you from here?" Lucas asked when he was finished recounting his own adventures.

Cady nodded. "My whole life is here," she replied. "For now."

As Cady reached over for more Cheetos, she accidentally stroked Lucas's knee and sensed instantly that Lucas liked being touched. He let his hand brush her knee, too, in that fake-accidental way that guys do to let you know they're interested.

With some more prompting, Cady launched into the quick version of her own life story. She told Lucas about her Colombian father and Irish mother and her pain-in-the-butt brother, Diego. She told him about studying for the SATs and then getting a 2000 and freaking out because that meant she would most likely get into the school of her choice. And then she told him that the school she really wanted to go to was Berklee College of Music.

For as good a talker as he was, Lucas was actually a good listener, too. His brown eyes did a lot of the work. Cady saw him glance from her face over to her guitar a few times. But it took him several minutes before he even mentioned the instrument.

"How long have you played?" Lucas asked, pointing to Fred.

"As long as I can remember."

"You know, I play, too," Lucas said.

"You do?" Cady was relieved—and more than a little bit excited—to know that they both played.

"I just play to keep myself sane. You know?" Lucas admitted.

Cady nodded. "Sure."

"I don't know if you're friends with the guy hosting this party," Lucas said, "but this music is really lame."

Cady cracked up. "I think Emile has this deluded fantasy that he's some kind of musical mix genius."

"Someone should throw the poor guy a buoy," Lucas said.

"He needs some more retro songs. They always work at parties."

"Exactly what I was thinking. Who wants to ring in the New Year with this top 40 stuff?"

Someone threw a cup across the room and a crowd of kids gasped. Punch splashed across one wall of the living room and across one guy's white T-shirt. He cursed and chased after the kid who'd thrown the cup.

"What would a party be without a little stupidity?" Cady asked.

Lucas shrugged. "I'm just the outsider, remember?" he said. "No comment."

"I see. . . ."

They both laughed.

Lucas's eyes darted back to the guitar again. Cady had a feeling that Lucas wanted to hold—or maybe even play—it. Her mind raced to think of the right words.

"You can open the case if you want," she finally said.

One invitation was all Lucas needed. He eagerly pulled out her Fender acoustic, pressing the frets.

"Go ahead," Cady said. "I don't mind if you play. My guitar looks good on you."

"Nah." Lucas sighed. "I haven't got any good songs in my head right now. Better off to wait until I can play you something really worthwhile. I mean, I want to impress you, right?"

Cady smiled warmly. "Right."

Lucas put the guitar back into the case and latched it shut. Then he looked up, listening to the song playing.

"Hey, now *this* is actually good. Maybe Emile heard what we said," Lucas said.

Cady shrugged. "Maybe."

"So," Lucas mused. "You been sitting here on this ugly couch all night?"

"Sort of," Cady said, giggling. She was tempted to come back with a line like: *Yeah, I was sitting here waiting for you, Lucas. I waited all last semester to get the chance to meet you just like this.* But instead, she said, "My friend Marisol came with me but she had to go home for something. I think she's coming back for the New Year's toast. Well, she better come back. She's my ride."

"So you're not here with your boyfriend or anything?" Lucas said.

"Boyfriend? Not exactly."

"Girlfriend?"

"Girlfriend?" Cady asked, surprised. "Not me."

"Well, then, maybe we can hang out a little bit more? You want a drink? I was feeling a little parched." Lucas stood up from the couch. "What can I get you?" he asked, his eyes inviting.

"Punch would be great."

"Great. Punch. Back in a flash."

Lucas walked away, and Cady couldn't help but check him out from behind. Marisol was always blabbing about how certain guys in their class were sexy, and Cady would always roll her eyes. But this guy was different. Where had he *been* all year? *All high school, that is?*

"Excuse me." Someone stepped in front of Cady, and she moved her legs and guitar case out of the way. Cady looked up to see Hope White standing there.

"Hello, Cady," Hope said.

Was that a sneer? Cady had given up trying to read all

of Hope's glacial facial expressions. Why did Hope always go out of her way to act mean around Cady and Cady's friends? After so long, Cady thought it was time to let go of old grudges. Senior year was halfway over. She wasn't going to let Hope ruin it for her.

"How are you, Hope?" Cady asked, smiling to herself. She wanted to give her enemy the benefit of the doubt.

But as usual Hope didn't answer. She disappeared swiftly around the other side of the sofa without even a glance.

Cady tried not to think about the snub. She turned her mind back to Lucas and hugged one of the pillows from the leather couch.

Her pulse raced. Cady's heart was way too full. Everything that had built up inside for so long came out like a song.

My heart's a drum
You are the one
My heart's a drum
You are the one
My heart's a drum
You are the one

The only thing Cady could do now was wait for Lucas. And see.

Ooh la la!

Don't miss

FRENCH KISS by Aimee Friedman —

the sizzling sequel to

the New York Times bestselling novel

SOUTH BEACH.

Available in bookstores everywhere!

Near midnight, Holly, Alexa, and Alexa's Parisian cousins, Raphaëlle and Pierre, headed straight to Eurotrash. Even on a Tuesday, the trendy Right Bank club boasted a mile-long line outside. But because Raphaëlle was buddies with the bouncer, he kissed her cheeks and lifted the velvet rope for her and her entourage.

Alexa felt a flutter of admiration for Raphaëlle as she followed her into the dark, pulsing nightclub. As a rule, Alexa wasn't easily bowled over by anyone, but she'd always been a little in awe of her eldest cousin, who — with her boho style and vivid personality — was the essence of individuality. Sometimes, around Raphaëlle, Alexa felt very much her mere eighteen years, and she couldn't help but wonder if — in her name-brand clothes and carefully applied makeup — she came off as just another high-maintenance, glossy American girl.

It wasn't a thought Alexa liked to dwell on.

Inside Eurotrash, Raphi flounced off to join her hipster friends, who were smoking at the serpentine chrome bar, leaving Alexa, Pierre, and Holly on the elevated platform above the dance floor. Alexa shed her sparkly shrug, soaking everything in: the strobe lights coloring the dance floor, the metallic silver couches strewn with kissing couples, and the floor-to-ceiling tinted windows that allowed clubgoers to stare out at the moonlit Champs-Elysées.

Alexa scanned the crowd and caught sight of a tall, lanky guy with a shaved head, wearing aviator shades and a ripped tee, amid swarms of other potential boy toys. She felt the delectable thrill of possibility. She'd forgotten how fun it was to be single. And, since she was conveniently in Paris — land of the *liasion* and home of the hottie — what better place was there to savor her new status?

Grabbing Holly's elbow, Alexa hollered over the pounding music: "Let's get two Stoli on the rocks and sandwich some cutie, okay?" She hoped poor Pierre wouldn't mind hanging alone. *Or,* she thought with a devilish smile, *he could come and dance with Holly.*

Holly pulled back, unsure. The dance floor was swarming with high-cheekboned, trendily outfitted club kids, and Holly suddenly felt very young, even in her chic new sea-green halter. Not to mention that she'd much rather dance to eighties songs — like pre-Kabbalah Madonna — than the house music blaring here. She'd had a blast clubbing in South Beach, but now that Holly had a boyfriend back home, she wouldn't feel too comfortable grinding with some anonymous European guy.

Shaking her head, she apologetically offered her still-sore ankle as an excuse. So Alexa shrugged, blew her and Pierre a kiss, and started off toward the bar, clearly on a boy-finding mission. Holly hoped Alexa knew what she was doing; she didn't think delving into a hookup right after a breakup was necessarily the best plan. But what did she know about boy stuff, really?

"Would you like to sit down?" Pierre asked. His hand on Holly's bare arm made her stomach jump. He gestured to the closest metallic couch, where two lanky boys lounged, sharing a cigarette. Holly agreed, and she and Pierre sat down on the opposite end from the boys. Since the couch wasn't that big, they had to sit sort of close together. Holly tried not to focus on the fact that Pierre's knee was kind of rubbing against hers as he leaned in and asked if she wanted a drink.

"No," Holly replied, too quickly. Then, as Pierre nodded and casually draped his arm over the back of the sofa, she understood that he hadn't been asking in a sketchy, I-want-to-get-you-drunk way — he'd simply noticed Holly's discomfort and was trying to break the ice. Holly glanced at Pierre and gave him a sheepish smile.

Pierre returned her smile, holding her gaze for a beat. "Your eyes," he said softly, still leaning close, his knee still touching hers. "They are a very nice green."

Holly shifted on the sofa, fighting down the beginnings of a deep blush. "Well, I think they're more gray-green," she replied, her tongue feeling clumsy in her mouth. Holly wasn't used to talking about her looks with anyone. When they were kissing, Tyler would sometimes pull back to study her face and whisper that she was pretty, but he'd never wax poetic on the exact shade of her eyes. "I mean, I guess their color depends on the weather," Holly rambled on, fiddling with her silver ring. "Or on my mood, or what I'm wearing, or . . ."

"This — how you say — shirt?" Pierre interjected, gently taking the hem of Holly's halter top and slowly rubbing it between his thumb and forefinger. "*Oui*. This shirt, it turns your eyes green."

"Um, yeah," Holly managed, acutely aware of Pierre's touch. She made a mental note to wear green for the rest of her stay in Paris; fortunately, Holly had added lots of that color to her wardrobe after a lime bikini had brought her very good luck last year.

Pierre removed his hand from her shirt and ran it through his dark curls. But his own beautiful eyes remained on Holly, almost as if — Holly barely dared entertain the thought — he couldn't get enough of looking at her. Holly wondered if it was possible to spontaneously combust from too much blushing in one night. *Must . . . change . . . the . . . subject*, she thought, her mind casting around wildly for something bland and basic to bring up. Something like . . . school.

"Pierre, what are you majoring in at the Sorbonne?" Holly blurted, not even bothering to try for a natural segue. Like any high school senior, Holly got border-line obsessed with anything college-related, so she *was* genuinely interested in Pierre's answer — especially if it took her mind off the fact that their arms were now pressing together. She leaned back against the sofa, willing herself to relax.

"Well, I think our system is a bit different from American universities," Pierre explained, his warm breath tickling her ear, "but I am studying law. It was my father's idea — I do not like it much." He rolled his eyes and Holly grinned, fully understanding that particular issue.

"Say no more," she replied, feeling her blush start to fade. "My parents want me to go to law school after college, too." She drew her finger across her throat in a kill-me-now motion, and Pierre cracked up. Holly felt a rush of warmth; she'd made him laugh. It was funny how a shared sense of humor could translate regardless of language boundaries.

"Talking about school," Pierre said (Holly wanted to correct him by saying "speaking of," but she held back; his malapropisms were too adorable), "I have no classes tomorrow." Pierre's hand, resting on the back of the couch, very lightly brushed the nape of Holly's neck. Though Holly tried to fight the feeling, tingles raced down her body. "Alexa tells me that this is your first time in Paris," he went on, his voice low. "So perhaps, 'Olly, you would enjoy it if I took you on a tour?"

Holly bit her lip, her heart pounding hard enough to be heard over the music. There were so many reasons for her to say no: She didn't know Pierre that well, she'd promised Alexa they would go shopping tomorrow, and, most important: Tyler, Tyler, and . . . Tyler. Holly felt bad enough as it was, sitting so close to a guy whose slightest touch turned her skin hot, who'd complimented her eyes, and who spoke her name so charmingly. Spending an entire day with him in the world's most romantic city might feel like mere heartbeats away from . . . *cheating*.

But Holly was frustrated with Tyler, who *still* hadn't called. And it wasn't like Pierre was a random sleaze who'd picked her up at Eurotrash; he was Alexa's sweet, smart cousin — and, Holly felt, a new friend. She'd be sorry to miss his take on Paris — which would surely prove more interesting than Alexa's overpriced shopping spree. So, without giving it another guilt-ridden thought, Holly turned to Pierre and smiled, watching as his blue eyes lit up hopefully.

And *that* felt like reason enough to tell him yes.

Stoli on the rocks in one hand, hips slowly swiveling to the music, Alexa was right where she wanted to be — smack in the middle of the throbbing Eurotrash dance floor. She'd just danced to Daft Punk's "One More Time" (the music that was hot in Europe was pretty much always played out in the States) with Aviator Boy, whose name, he'd whispered to her, was Jean-Claude. But before Jean-Claude could start kissing her, Alexa had decided there were tastier options to explore — shaved heads didn't really do it for her — and waved him off.

A sudden pair of hands on her waist didn't surpise

Alexa too much. Even in her plain black dress, she was confident she looked as sultry as any of the international supermodels working it on the dance floor.

And when Alexa turned around, a supermodel was what she saw.

He had lush, white-blond hair that swept sexily over one eye and fell in waves to his square chin. The eye not hidden by the sweep of hair was a deep midnight blue, and fringed with the darkest, longest lashes Alexa had ever seen on a guy. His jaw-dropping body looked familiar, and Alexa whirred through the boy-Rolodex in her mind — *Did he kiss me in Cannes when I was fifteen? Hit on me in an Amsterdam bar two summers ago? Walk the runway at Fashion Week in New York last year?* — until she realized she'd seen him that very afternoon. While Alexa was on her way to meet Holly, he'd pouted at her — shirtless — from a billboard above the Métro station.

But glimpsing Model Boy in the flesh was much, much nicer.

They started dancing, his hands on her waist, her free hand on his shoulder as she held on to her drink. Their bodies moved sinuously together. Alexa threw her head back, her hair rippling down to her waist, and she laughed as Model Boy leaned in to touch his lips to her neck. She'd done it — she'd snagged the most beautiful guy in all of Eurotrash.

Model Boy took Alexa's head in his hands and tilted her back up so they were eye to eye. "I'm Sven," he whispered, giving her a big-toothed smile. "*Parlez-vous* — uh, *anglais?*" Over the music, Alexa could make out a trace of a Swedish accent.

Alexa's heart leaped; so Sven assumed she was French! Who said male models were dumb? Beaming, Alexa slid her arms around Sven's neck, slipping her free hand beneath the collar of his sheer, fitted black shirt. Alexa reflected that, in the States, no straight boy would be caught dead in what Sven was wearing. But she knew, from the way he was gripping her hips, that Sven couldn't be gay — he was just European. By now, Alexa had learned to spot the difference.

"Alexa," she whispered, standing on her tiptoes so her lips touched Sven's perfect earlobe. "And I do speak English. But we won't be talking much, will we?"

Taking her cue — *he's practically a genius!* Alexa thought — Sven lowered his face and kissed her, soft and deep. Delighting in the feel of his lips on hers, Alexa moved her hand to the back of Sven's head, intensifying the kiss. A second later, though, some of Sven's hair got into her mouth, so Alexa pulled back, giggling and wiping her lips. *The perils of kissing a long-haired boy.* Normally, when fooling around, Alexa liked to be the one with the hair dramatically spilling everywhere. Maybe a guy with a shaved head would actually have been better.

"Watch it," Sven chided her, shaking his luscious locks back into place.

Alexa couldn't tell if he was joking or not, but, growing more turned off by the second, she watched as Sven reached into the back pocket of his jeans and pulled out a handheld mirror. Frowning into it, he fussed with his hair, making sure each golden strand was back in place. Then Sven ran a discerning finger over one of his arched eyebrows and puckered his lips at the mirror, as if he'd rather be kissing it than Alexa.

Oh my God, Alexa realized, her stomach plummeting in disbelief. *He's even more vain than . . . me.*

When Sven was finally finished examining his stunning self, he tucked the mirror away and pulled Alexa in for another long kiss. But this time, Alexa didn't move her lips in response, so Sven pulled back and flashed her a pinup-worthy grin.

"Oh, *I* get it, Vanessa," he said, tossing his hair as if he were in a shampoo commercial. "You are, ah, afraid you'll get too carried away by kissing me."

"It's Alexa," Alexa replied, through gritted teeth.

"So come back to my place," Sven continued obliviously. "I'm staying at the Ritz-Carlton. I have a photo shoot in the Bois du Boulogne early tomorrow morning, but we can still party all night." Then he fluttered his lashes at her — which, Alexa realized, was her signature come-hither move. This was all wrong.

Alexa wasn't sure if it was all the champagne she'd had at dinner, the vodka she was drinking now, or the fact that Sven was Narcissus come to life, but suddenly she felt sick to her stomach. A year ago, Alexa knew she would have *jumped* at the chance to spend the night at the Ritz-Carlton with a Swedish supermodel. But now, the thought of a one-night stand with Sven wasn't sitting right with her at all. *Maybe I'm more mature than I was back then*, Alexa thought, removing her arms from around Sven's neck and rattling the cubes in her glass of Stoli.

Or maybe she just couldn't bring herself to hook up with a boy who was prettier than she was.